DEATH DOWN THE AISLE

BOOK SEVEN

EMILY QUEEN

Death Down the Aisle

ISBN- 978-1-953044-91-4

First Edition

Printed in the U.S.A.

Table of Contents

CHAPTER ONE

Rosemary Lillywhite shoved her way into her London townhouse and heaved a sigh of relief when the butler, Wadsworth, deftly divested her of an armload of packages. She thanked him, noted a slight furrowing of his brow, and grimaced apologetically for what felt like the thousandth time in three months.

He hurried off without engaging in any sort of discussion; there was no need, as he and his mistress knew they were indeed on the same side of the losing battle.

As she hung her coat on a rack near the front door, Rosemary appraised the state of the foyer with a scowl of her own—making no attempt to hide her irritation as Wadsworth had so politely done.

Overflowing crates piled high on either side of the hallway threatened to topple as she brushed past. His frame not nearly as slim as Rosemary's, Wadsworth had,

1

no doubt, been forced to turn sideways to get to the front door—an affront, she was sure, to his butlering sensibilities.

In January, at the beginning of the siege, there had been some sort of order to the chaos. Now with the spring season underway, crates labeled with such trivialities as "scarves" and "spring handbags" mingled with those containing all manner of wedding supplies, the whole lot of it coated in a web-like layer of snowy white tulle.

When she'd assured her best friend, Vera Blackburn—who was slated to be married to Rosemary's brother, Frederick, in little more than a week—that temporarily sharing the large townhouse would be no imposition whatsoever, she hadn't realized she'd also been offering to store everything both Vera and Frederick owned.

Frederick was one thing; he tended to travel lightly, but Vera was another story altogether. Of course, Rosemary had known better than anyone how much Vera enjoyed shopping—she simply hadn't realized that her friend never got rid of anything.

How it had all fit into Vera's old flat was a mystery, and one even Frederick seemed unwilling to address. He had, however, begun searching for a larger marital home than originally planned.

As content as she'd been to have the two of them stay with her, the offer had less to do with a desire for companionship than it did with keeping the family peace. Rosemary's mother, Evelyn, had very nearly swooned when she'd discovered Frederick and Vera's plans to live together before their official wedding day.

That they were sleeping in the same bedroom at Rosemary's townhouse didn't seem to make much difference to Evelyn, or perhaps she simply presumed otherwise.

What went on behind closed doors was of little interest—appearance was what mattered, particularly to her mother's high-society friends, and it was their opinion that fueled Evelyn's desires.

Whether she agreed with that outlook or not was of little consequence. Evelyn cared, and despite her somewhat prickly nature, Rosemary adored her mother and wanted her to be pleased. And so, she had intervened, reinforcing the fragile peace that had only recently developed between Vera and her future mother-in-law.

Vera agreed to let her have a heavy hand in planning the wedding, and Evelyn—well, to be fair, Evelyn hadn't agreed to much beyond a vague promise not to completely take over and dominate the preparations.

Rosemary suspected she'd had her fingers crossed behind her back all the while because it hadn't, of course, taken long for her efforts to dissolve.

The first disagreement over whether lily or rose

centerpieces were more appropriate had drawn another line in the sand, and the temperature of the relationship had fluctuated wildly ever since.

It wasn't so much that Evelyn disliked Vera or thought she wasn't good enough for her precious boy—although it had seemed that way at first, particularly from Vera's perspective. She simply didn't get on with the radical notions of the day's youth, many of which Vera proudly represented.

Evelyn would have been utterly shocked to learn that when it came right down to brass tacks, her morals and values weren't so very far from Vera's after all. They'd made strides, and Rosemary suspected that after the wedding planning process was over—an experience already fraught with tension under normal circumstances—her mother and Vera would find a great deal more common ground.

After all, there'd never been another woman who'd adored Frederick as much as Evelyn; not until Vera, and that would certainly, Rosemary hoped, earn her some points in Evelyn's estimation.

Now, from down the hall, Rosemary could hear Frederick's voice and was alarmed to note that he sounded angry. Given her brother's general joviality, it raised Rosemary's hackles, and she quickened her pace. A sharp retort from Vera caused her to stop short of entering the parlor door as intended. Instead, she paused to listen—quite unashamedly, as it was, after all, her own house.

"I've had enough," Frederick replied. "I can't live a lie any longer. It would only be a mistake. Can't you see that?"

"No," Vera breathed, her voice filled with a mixture of anger, pain, and betrayal so palpable it caused Rosemary's chest to constrict and her heart to race. "You said you loved me—that you always had and always would. How can it all be over?"

Frederick groaned, and by the sound of it, kicked something—Rosemary hoped, through her dismay, it hadn't been the chintz footstool that had belonged to her late husband's mother—and when he spoke again, he sounded tired.

"Can we please just be finished? Truly, Vera, I don't have anything more in me."

At that, Rosemary rounded the corner and shoved a pointed finger in her brother's face. "What exactly do you think you're doing, Frederick Woolridge? You will not break Vera's heart, do you hear me? You're right lucky she's willing to put up with you for the rest of her life! Do you think you can find better? Is that it?" She demanded, placing her hands on her hips and glaring at him in dismay.

"What? Rosie, no!" Frederick yelped, looking to Vera with a panicked expression. "It's not what you think!"

Rosemary's gaze shifted to Vera, whose face had turned a rosy shade of red, her eyes filling with tears.

"Oh, Vera, don't cry. It will be all right," Rosemary said, rushing forward.

Before she could get to her, Vera burst out laughing and collapsed onto the sofa. "Rosie," she stuttered, trying to find her breath.

"Here, sister dear," Frederick said dryly, handing Rosemary a battered bundle of bound papers. She didn't have to more than glance at them to realize her mistake.

"I'm just running lines with our resident actress. I've certainly no intention of jilting poor Vera, though it's lovely to know whose side you would take in the event we decided to part ways."

Rosemary flung the script onto the settee, narrowly missing Vera's prone but still heaving form, and poured herself a brandy. "It's always the man's fault, didn't you know that, Freddie? You're fortunate, really, since you're already so thoroughly used to being wrong."

Her tone had a significantly rougher edge to it than usual, and Rosemary felt an immediate rush of remorse as her brother's eyebrows drew together.

"Swell, Rose, really," he said with a low whistle.

"What's got you all in a lather?"

"Charming, indeed, Frederick," she retorted, suddenly less contrite than she'd been a moment ago.

His cheerful mood returning, Frederick winked. "The skirts do, on the whole, seem to find me irresistible."

Vera snorted, rolled her eyes, and made room on the settee for her friend. "It's a good thing our parents have already spent a small fortune on this wedding," she said, though there was little genuine irritation in her tone, and her eyes twinkled when they met Frederick's gaze. "It would be a pity to reconsider now. Whatever would happen to all the gifts that have already been bought on our behalf?"

Rosemary pressed her lips together, her eyes rolling skyward. "How you truly do find him charming is beyond me," she remarked wryly.

She'd be pleased as punch when her brother and Vera were finally off on their post-wedding holiday, and she wouldn't have to watch them moon over one another for a few blissful weeks.

The thought conjured an image from the last holiday the three of them had taken when they'd all become involved in a murder investigation and nearly killed, and once more, she felt ashamed for snapping. If anything happened to either Frederick or Vera during their travels, she hadn't a clue what she'd do with herself.

"Apologies. I don't know why I feel so at odds these days," Rosemary explained.

"Perhaps, Rosie, you're tired of navigating a labyrinth every time you enter the foyer," Frederick said wryly. "We're all on edge, and we all want to get this whole thing done and over with."

For that, he received a sharp look from his fiancee and quickly tried to backtrack, mumbling something about "a most special day" until Vera waved a hand to indicate he was better off not speaking at all.

She turned to Rosemary and squeezed her friend's hand. "He's right, you know, for once. We aren't blind to the fact our being here—with all our earthly belongings—is an inconvenience. We'd intended to tell you over dinner, but I suppose now is as good a time as any," she said, sharing a conspiratorial look with Frederick.

"We've finally settled on a place—the one six streets down with the gorgeous coving—and Frederick is working double-time to ensure it's ready as soon as possible. This is likely our last night here, so you needn't fret any longer. Tomorrow we leave for Pardington, and of course, we'll spend the week there preparing for the wedding. After the party, we catch a train to our destination, and by the time we return, the house ought to be finished and fully furnished. Isn't that fantastic?"

This all had tumbled excitedly out of Vera's mouth

with barely a breath in between.

The news did, in fact, lift a weight off Rosemary's chest, and a smile lit her face as she sprang from the settee. "This calls for a toast and a nice dinner out. Freddie, go fetch some champagne out of the icebox, and I'll call Kettner's and see if they can get us in at the last minute."

Frederick rolled his eyes and shook his head. "You get the champagne; I'll call Kettner's. I've got connections, now, you know."

"All right, brother, point taken," Rosemary grinned and changed trajectory. On her way out of the parlor, she heard Vera ask, "What connections?" to which Frederick puffed up his chest and replied, "I practically run the London branch of Woolridge & Sons, don't I? The job does happen to come with a few perks."

Rosemary shook her head as she made her way to the kitchen and back, thinking how terribly funny it was how life tended to turn out the exact opposite of how one expected it would.

A few short years ago, she wouldn't have imagined Frederick bragging about a position at their father's company. He had, on more than one occasion, vehemently insisted the job would be an utter bore. He'd no reason whatsoever to become gainfully employed when there was more than enough family money to go around.

Then again, she never imagined him marrying Vera—or settling down with anyone at all, for that matter—proving that people, even Freddie, were capable of change.

Perhaps, she mused, even Evelyn would also come around one day and begin to accept her childrens' choices with a modicum of understanding and acceptance.

Or, perhaps, pigs would fly.

CHAPTER TWO

When she returned to the parlor, the dinner reservation had already been made and jaunty jazz emitted from the wireless. Vera sprawled against the back of the settee, her long, shapely legs tucked beneath her, a cigarette in a gold-plated holder in one hand and a crystal highball glass in the other.

She looked alarmingly like her mother, bright, emerald eyes framed by a fringe of raven hair and a stunning figure. Lorraine Blackburn had been a shining star of the stage when she was Vera's age. Both women possessed the ability to command a room with little effort.

"We've called in reinforcements, Rosie," Vera shouted over the din. "*Chief Inspector Whittington* is on his way." She winked one wide, kohl-lined eye and wiggled her brows.

Maximilian Whittington—simply Max to his

friends—was the only man Rosemary had even considered dating since her husband's death the year before, even though his prior position as Andrew's best mate had given the romance a somewhat awkward start.

They'd moved past that now, and Max had become such a fixture in her life and in her home that he no longer bothered to ring the doorbell. It irritated Wadsworth, who considered his butlering duties not only sacred but paramount to keeping a proper home, to no end.

And so when, some time later, Max entered the parlor with absolutely no warning and carrying a note that must have been left at the front door, Rosemary knew Wadsworth was likely seething with irritation.

The next time he got her alone, she had a feeling she'd be treated to a lecture on allowing him to do his job. She knew that lecture by heart and would have preferred to avoid another rousing rendition.

Rosemary jumped up from her perch on the edge of the footstool that Frederick had, thankfully, spared during his moment of irritation earlier in the evening and planted an enthusiastic kiss square on Max's lips.

"We've requested to be seated in the champagne bar, and our reservation is in twenty minutes. I hope you're feeling peckish—" Rosemary stopped short, noting the pinched expression on his face. "What's wrong?"

"I think it would be best to reconsider our plans for the evening, Rose," he replied, handing her the envelope.

Rosemary took it and flipped it over. Then, when she saw the symbol scrawled across the back, promptly dropped it on the floor as if it had suddenly caught fire. Her hand shook as she bent to pick the envelope back up, a cold chill trailing up her spine and turning her blood to ice.

"What is it, Rosie?" Vera shouted just as Frederick flipped off the music, the commotion drawing Wadsworth from wherever he had been lurking. He stood at the door, his eyes trained on his mistress, an expression of concern etched across his face.

"It's from Garrison Black," Rosemary explained, deadpan, her gaze rising to meet not her friend who had asked the question, but Wadsworth, who for once wasn't able to quickly arrange his features into a mask of reassuring calm.

Vera let out a hiss and Frederick a short but descriptive expletive while Rosemary steeled herself and ripped open the envelope. Two splotches of color appeared high on otherwise pale cheeks as her eyes narrowed and her back went ramrod straight.

She handed the card back to Max and allowed the lot of them to look over his shoulder, Wadsworth nearly snatching it from his hands but thinking better of such a blatant display of disrespect.

"It seems I'm his next target," Rosemary pronounced matter-of-factly and then perched on the edge of settee and resumed sipping her brandy. Now, her hands were rock-steady.

Max rounded on Rosemary, seeming to take the words right out of Wadsworth's mouth, judging by the expression on his face. "You don't sound particularly concerned, Rosemary," he accused. "Are you in shock?"

"I'm not in shock," Rosemary replied serenely. "I'm angry if you want to know the truth. So angry I could spit, but what would that accomplish? Regardless, I refuse to give this man any more power than he already believes he has."

Vera gawked at her friend. "I'm all for standing up to one's enemies, Rosie, but Garrison Black is a mass murderer, and you're just his type!"

It was true, Rosemary possessed the blond hair and blue eyes Black preferred, but so did any number of women in London. She was older than his usual victims by almost a decade; he liked them no older than twenty, but Rosemary suspected he'd make an exception on that front. She lived alone—at least she usually did—making her an easier target in Black's twisted mind.

The reason, Rosemary knew, she found herself in a killer's sights had more to do with ego than anything else. Black was, after all, a prideful man. A psychotic, prideful man—not an encouraging combination—and she had, effectively, taken his last potential victim out of the running. Unless, of course, he wanted to fly across the Atlantic to kill Arabelle Grey.

"Did I somehow imply that I'm going to lie down and die?" She knew she probably oughtn't to have phrased it quite that way, but Rosemary found she cared little for what was proper or sensitive at that moment. "I'm quite certain neither Max nor Wadsworth will allow anything terrible to befall me."

Wadsworth stretched up to his full height and nodded once at Rosemary. "Of course not, Miss Rose. I'll protect you with my life."

"Well, I'm glad that's settled. Shall we all head off to Kettner's then?" Rosemary asked, rising from her spot on the sofa and downing the rest of her brandy.

She realized as she watched her friends stare at her with variations of incredulity and irritation—each of which caused a giggle to rise into her throat—that perhaps she was in shock after all. Garrison Black was no laughing matter.

"He's already murdered six women and a police officer, avoided being incarcerated for ten years, and then managed to escape when the London constabulary finally successfully captured him!" Frederick ran through the high points of Black's escapades, none of which was news to anyone, particularly Rosemary.

Black was, now, still on the loose, and judging by the contents of the card that had just arrived, he'd decided to take his anger out on Rosemary.

She didn't want to look at the card again, despite her steady hand. Didn't want to see the sketch of Arabelle Grey gazing into a mirror with Rosemary's own face looking back.

She definitely didn't want to admit that Black, despite his status as a deranged lunatic, was a gifted artist and had captured both their faces in exquisite detail. And she absolutely did not want to read the note at the bottom, punctuated by Black's signature black heart symbol that made Rosemary's stomach turn.

Bloody art thou, bloody will be thy end, it read. She recognized the Shakespearean quote and held no illusions as to what it meant. Garrison Black didn't appreciate her meddling and had vowed to make her pay.

"Have you gone mad, Rosie?" Frederick finally asked after engaging in a silent battle with Max, who appeared somewhat reluctant to stoke the flames of Rosemary's fire, no matter how reduced to coals it might seem.

He knew from experience it only took one spark to reignite her fury, and he'd nearly decided to take his lumps after all when Frederick took the bullet. "Haven't you been listening to anything Max has said for the last two months?"

She had, actually, been riveted by Max's recounting of the investigation into Black's past. It had been a set of notes left behind by the late Sergeant Nathaniel Prescott that sparked Max to look at the Black case differently—a set of notes and some encouragement by Rosemary herself, who couldn't help wonder why Black had done what he did. She remembered every detail but allowed Frederick to run through the fine points anyway.

"Garrison Black is deranged. That Freud chap must be having a field day with his story: left to rot by his father, beaten by his mother, and held in contempt by just about everyone during his school days. He's angry, delusional, and isn't capable of remorse for the pain he's inflicted upon his victims. What's worse, once he's decided on a target, he won't stop until she's dead."

Hearing Freddie—*always look on the bright side of life* Freddie—recount the information in such detail, proving he had indeed been closely following the Black case with worry brought the whole thing into perspective. Suddenly, Rosemary sank back onto the sofa and held her hands aloft. "What shall we do, then?"

"Take any and all precautions at our disposal," Max declared. "Luckily, you're all heading off to Pardington tomorrow. I'll assign extra patrols in the area while you're gone."

"I shall drive Miss Rosemary to Pardington," Wadsworth said in a firm tone. "Then return to keep an eye on the house."

Max shook his head. "Thank you, Wadsworth, but I believe it will be safer all round if Rosemary were to wait until Sunday and drive up with me."

Wadsworth nodded and gave way without argument.

"I'm perfectly capable of driving myself, you know," Rosemary insisted. But Max would not be moved, and besides, there were the other women of her household to consider.

Anna, Rosemary's young lady's maid, was naught but a girl and just as sweet as could be; Gladys had only recently come into employ, but she'd endeared herself quickly. Neither woman was Rosemary willing to sacrifice or compromise.

"Thank you, Wadsworth," Rosemary smiled at the man who was more than simply an employee. He'd become family to her and knew exactly how to ease her mind.

"I trust," Wadsworth said to Max, "you will see her safely home."

"Count on it," Max said. A wordless understanding passed between the two men. If Rosemary had been paying more attention, she might have taken umbrage.

With her plans settled, Rosemary forced her attention down a practical, domestic path, finding that focusing on the mundane made the whole situation a little less horrific.

"Come, Vera. Let's put this out of our heads and slip into the old glad rags. I'm positively famished." That was a lie, as her appetite had all but fled. "We wouldn't want to miss our reservation."

Chapter Three

When Rosemary arrived at her parent's house in Pardington on Sunday morning, she hadn't expected to be shooed, unceremoniously, right back out the door. Frederick had answered the bell ahead of the butler, Mr. Geoffrey—an unusual feat, but not entirely unprecedented—amid what sounded like a boisterous gathering of inebriated men.

"To the billiards room!" a raucous call to arms wafted from somewhere inside the house, and Rosemary's eyes went saucer-wide when she realized it had come from her little cousin, Timmy, who'd been a mere boy when she'd last laid eyes on him. Now, he had a thin mustache adorning his upper lip, and his torso had finally grown into his gangly limbs.

Frederick hollered back that he'd be right along, then pulled the door closed far enough to block Rosemary's view.

"Didn't you get my message, Rosie? The ladies of the family are all bunking at the Blackburn estate; we men have taken over Woolridge House. Max, you're to stay with us. Now, Rose, shoo and let me enjoy my last days of freedom."

Rosemary raised an eyebrow, and her arms, backing away in retreat. "I'll pass that message along to your betrothed," she said devilishly. "Not that I expect you'll survive long enough to pay the price. Mother will have you drawn and quartered when you don't show up for Sunday service. You'd better hope she doesn't stop by on her way back to the Blackburn estate for some forgotten item."

Frederick swallowed hard, shot his sister a scathing look, and then retreated inside, leaving the door cracked open for Max.

"I suppose I'll leave you to it, then. Quite good luck we chose to bring my car." It hadn't been luck exactly, as Rosemary satisfied her impatience with the late start by ordering Wadsworth to load her things ahead as she wanted to be ready the moment Max arrived.

"I'll see you…later?" Max sounded unsure of his prospects because the drive to Pardington hadn't gone exactly to his plan. Rosemary had flatly refused to discuss Garrison Black, his card, or Max's ideas on handling the threat.

"Better go with *eventually*. I've no clue what Frederick has in store for you, but it will likely be far more entertaining than the Sunday sermon," she declared wistfully before bidding him goodbye. It wouldn't do to keep Evelyn waiting, particularly not now that only Rosemary would attend the service.

Frederick owed her more than he realized, and she tucked the thought away, vowing not only to make him pay but to wait for the most inconvenient time to collect.

"Rose, wait," a voice called to her when she was halfway back to her car. She turned and was pleased to see another of her cousins, Simon, emerging from the front door. He took a careful look around as though he were doing something he oughtn't to have been and jogged over to her. "Mind giving me a lift to the church?"

Rosemary noted that he'd got himself all gussied up, his Patent Leather hair combed meticulously into position and held in place with a liberal coating of Brilliantine.

"Don't you look handsome," Rosemary said, motioning for him to come along and get into the passenger seat.

Simon was the oddest of the cousins and the one Frederick had been most reluctant to include in the pre-wedding festivities. Stella, their younger sister, shared Frederick's irritation, primarily due to Simon's uncanny and unintentional knack for getting Stella into hot water.

Being the eldest (in addition to the oddest), it fell to Simon to mind the younger cousins while the aunts and uncles socialized. On his first visit to Woolridge House, he bet a gullible Stella she couldn't climb to the top of Evelyn's prized china cabinet.

Possessed of an uncommon curiosity and not one single ounce of caution, Stella, of course, immediately accepted the challenge. When she stranded herself at the top, Simon bolted before the adults saw him and had a chance to decide he'd been derelict in his duty.

Frederick managed to drag a dining room chair in front of the cabinet and get her down, but her dismount jostled the cabinet, resulting in one of Evelyn's prized teacups losing its handle.

Both equally considered the brains of the caper, Stella and Frederick bore the brunt of Evelyn's displeasure. They'd both been understandably soured towards their older cousin, and thus, it had fallen to Rosemary to act as the more charitable Woolridge sibling.

As a result, she and Simon had developed a special

bond, and she truly was delighted to see him.

"I thought it best not to arouse the wrath of Aunt Evelyn," Simon explained. "Who else will be in attendance?" The pink tint of his cheeks gave away the real reason he'd decided to brave the ridicule of the rest of the men in the family and attend church along with the women—and why he'd felt it necessary to sneak past Frederick in order to do so.

The reason was, as it always had been, Vera. Simon had been smitten for as long as Rosemary could remember. It didn't seem to make any difference that he was several years younger than her, or that she'd never shown an inkling of interest—or even that she was, in exactly one week, intending to marry his older cousin.

"You'll keep your status as her favorite nephew, certainly. You might even take Frederick's place at the top of mother's nice list." It was a position Freddie maintained with great precariousness.

At that, Simon smiled widely, looking for a moment like his boyish self.

She thought about slipping him a silent warning but ultimately decided not to press the matter. If Simon wished to have his heart repeatedly crushed under Vera's stiletto heel, that was his business. Instead, they spent the short ride to the church chatting about

Simon's spring travel plans, leaving Rosemary wondering why every time she turned around, someone in her circle had decided to go flitting off across the pond.

Positioned not far from Woolridge House and directly adjacent to the Blackburn estate's rear garden, the chapel's convenient proximity had been a point in its favor—and also one against—when Mrs. Blackburn presented Vera with the idea of holding the ceremony there.

Vera would have preferred a swanky London ballroom for the event, and Rosemary had expected her mother to agree without argument, but Lorraine Blackburn would hear none of it. Vera protested; Lorraine pressed, and finally, reinforcements had been called in.

Evelyn, never one to refuse her most prized pal's requests, insisted that her son simply must be married in the family church and subtly implied that Vera would lose favor if she refused to comply.

Suffice it to say, Vera had agreed against two-to-one odds, but only begrudgingly, and she'd carried on until Rosemary had finally had enough. After all, she'd explained to Vera, it could certainly have been worse: her mother could have chosen the other church in Pardington—the one behind which she and

Vera were once held at gunpoint by a deranged killer!

They also could have searched the entire English countryside and still not have found a more picturesque location for her special day. Set against a backdrop of rolling, patchwork hills, the modest wattle-and-daub church boasted an ornately carved steeple quaintly reminiscent of one of Oxford's celebrated spires.

As Evelyn had always been an active parishioner, Rosemary remembered playing in the small garden outside the vicarage—a small thatch-roofed cottage positioned catty-corner from the church building proper—as her mother and the vicar's wife enjoyed tea and conversation.

Having arrived with a few scant minutes to spare, Rosemary stood just inside the door and appraised the view of the sanctuary. Her mother and Lorraine Blackburn sat in a pew two rows back from the pulpit, their heads bent together, engaged in an intense discussion about what topic Rosemary had no desire to discover.

Stella leaned back in her seat, looking miserably uncomfortable on the hard wooden pew. She felt a pang of pity for poor, swollen-bellied Stella, but the feeling fled quickly as she wistfully imagined the little bundle of joy her sister would get to bring home in a few short months.

Finally, Rosemary caught sight of Vera, seated in the center of the bride's side of the nave. Vera peered up at one of the stained-glass windows with a furrowed brow, which smoothed when she noticed Rosemary standing at the back of the church.

With Simon following so closely she could all but feel his breath on her neck, Rosemary made her way down the aisle and thanked several saints when her young cousin chose to sit with Evelyn.

Out of the corner of her eye, Rosemary noticed his flushed countenance and the way his face reddened when Vera smiled in his direction. Distracted, the poor besotted boy managed to nearly knock the hat off the woman seated at the end of the pew.

"What are you doing?" Rosemary asked when she'd shimmied into the seat next to her friend.

Vera scowled. "I'm trying to decide whether there's too much red in that window with the portrait of Mary. The light is shining almost directly onto the spot where we'll be standing during the ceremony." She pointed towards the pulpit at a spot of dappled light no bigger than a hatbox. "I don't want my dress to look pink, now do I?"

Rosemary blinked a couple of times in quick

succession and bit back a sassy remark. "I'm not sure there's much of anything to be done about it."

"There must be something. Perhaps they could paint it a different color."

"Are you mad?" Rosemary kept her voice low, received a sharp look in response. "And who are *they* exactly?"

"I'm not *mad*, Rosie. I simply cannot walk down the aisle looking like a strawberry. That won't do at all," Vera lamented, stopping just short of a wail as she noticed an elderly lady in the row behind glaring in her direction.

"It's ten o'clock in the morning, Vera," Rosemary hissed in a stage whisper, "and your ceremony isn't until one in the afternoon. The sun won't even be in the same spot by then, so why don't you worry about something that actually matters, like whether your bobby pins are the right length?"

Sarcasm was lost on Vera at that moment because she didn't crack a smile or elbow Rosemary in the ribs as she usually would have done in response to the cheeky comment. "There's plenty to worry about," she said instead, deadly serious. "The frizz, for one thing."

"The what?" Rosemary asked, no clue what her friend was talking about.

"Hy's frizz," Vera replied, staring at Rosemary as though that ought to be all the explanation required. When she continued to stare blankly, Vera delivered the elbow jab Rosemary had been waiting for.

"Look," Vera said, pointing towards the front of the church, to where a line of young ladies sat in the pew behind her mother and Rosemary's. "My cousin, Hyacinth, the ginger-haired one. If it rains—as it has been doing on and off for days now—she will walk down the aisle looking like a shaving brush in a fancy dress."

Rosemary grimaced, and then suddenly, she vividly remembered a little girl with ginger pigtails from the annual Blackburn family gatherings. "That's little Hy? She's grown up, hasn't she? I believe we're getting old, Vera."

She dodged the elbow jab she'd been waiting for and then took a closer look at the girls huddled near Hyacinth. "That one's Delilah, isn't she?" Rosemary asked, indicating the most fair-skinned of them all, a willowy slip of a thing with thick auburn hair.

"Looks a little different now, doesn't she?"

"She's really grown into those teeth," Rosemary replied. "Lucky girl."

Vera snorted. "Quite so, and lucky for me too, since she's to be the other one of my bridesmaids. I'd have had nary a decent photograph of my wedding had nature not smiled upon the poor thing." She grimaced as if just now realizing perhaps church wasn't the place for such a comment and hurried to add, "She's turning into a lovely young lady—they both are."

The noise level in the cathedral decreased abruptly as the vicar, thin to the point of gauntness and favoring one leg, approached the pulpit. Father Dawson smiled, his face so round and cheerful, it almost looked as if his head were attached to the wrong body.

"Who's the one with the jet-black hair?" Rosemary asked in a stage whisper, referring to the last of the trio of girls seated in the front pew.

"Oh, she's not one of ours. That's Belle Dawson," Vera replied under her breath, "I presume. The vicar's daughter. Delilah and Hy spent all last evening discussing what a lucky girl she is. Apparently," Vera pointed towards the seat where an earnest-looking young man sat staring raptly at Father Dawson, "She's set to marry that tow-headed fellow. As he's just been ordained, it seems she'll be moving from one vicarage to another once he's received his formal posting."

From a distance, the new vicar hardly looked old enough to carry the title. Vera must have been of the same mind as she whispered, "Honestly, it took a great effort for me to keep my opinion to myself. I wanted to scream, 'don't marry the first boy who comes along! Live a little bit of life before you tie yourself down.' I didn't say any of that, of course. It's none of my nevermind, surely. And even if it were, it wouldn't help. He's attractive enough in a boyish sort of way. They're all besotted with him."

All three of the girls practically vibrated with excitement. Rosemary could see that even from ten rows back. Every few moments, Belle, seated in the middle, would lean to one side or another and make a comment out of the corner of her mouth, causing the other two to titter.

Father Dawson, either having grown accustomed to his daughter's behavior or simply not noticing, continued on with his sermon. Rosemary noted that he was actually nowhere near as dull as she'd expected him to be. Unfortunately, she had only managed to absorb a few minor points given Vera's constant stream of whispered chatter.

"Just look now, would you?" Vera spoke in Rosemary's ear at the beginning of the second round of hymns.

The dreaded red beam of light now decorated the vicar's white robe, and Vera looked as if she might go apoplectic as a result. It took Rosemary stomping on Vera's foot to quell the commentary as it slowly traveled up to his forehead.

After the sermon was over, and the crowd had dispersed, Rosemary caught up with Evelyn and Stella while Vera waylaid her mother and forced Lorraine to evaluate the stained-glass window she still fretted over.

"Mother," Rosemary said, kissing Evelyn on the cheek and then embracing her sister with enthusiasm. "Stella, look at you! You're positively glowing."

Stella smiled back thinly and replied, "Yes, it's an absolute joy. I couldn't be happier."

When their mother broke away searching for Lorraine Blackburn, Stella leaned in closer to Rosemary. "That was an absolute *lie*. I'm miserable, but anytime I say anything negative about this pregnancy, Mother goes off on a tangent about the wonders of motherhood. Father told me she was a holy terror with every single one of us, and to ignore her, so I've decided to take his advice and get back at her by naming the baby something she'll absolutely despise!"

Rosemary threw her head back in a laugh and linked arms with Stella. "How very proud Freddie shall be of his little sister."

"Freddie will be lucky to survive the evening, skipping church," Stella smirked. "Simon is off the hook, but the rest of that lot is in big trouble unless we find a way to distract her."

"I think Vera has a plan for doing just that," Rosemary said, pointing across the church to where Evelyn stood next to Lorraine, the pair of them exchanging incredulous looks while Vera gesticulated wildly at the stained-glass window.

The vicar stood some feet away, listening patiently. Rosemary pulled Stella along beside her and approached the group just in time to hear him say, "My dear child, I assure you, your wedding service will be beautiful. Don't fret, now."

"Thank you, Father Dawson," Vera finally acquiesced after a few more exchanges during which the vicar repeated the same soothing platitudes. "Perhaps you've a point, and the sun won't be in the same place it is now during the ceremony."

Of course, the vicar was right, Rosemary thought, exasperated. It was the same thing she'd said to Vera, not an hour earlier, and yet it seemed her reassurance had gone in one ear and out the other.

And then, as if she'd read Rosemary's mind and

felt the need to prove her wrong, Vera added, "All the same, I think I'll come back tomorrow and make doubly sure. You won't mind, will you?"

CHAPTER FOUR

"Rosemary!" Lorraine Blackburn mercifully interrupted, shouting loud enough to shatter the glass windows Vera was so troubled over. She came across the aisle to wrap Rosemary in a tight embrace, kissing her enthusiastically on both cheeks. "You look positively marvelous, darling!"

The cloying scent of expensive French perfume invaded Rosemary's nose, threatened to overwhelm her senses, but she inhaled deeply anyway. It was easy, maybe even necessary, to, in her absence, forget the intensity of the force that was Lorraine. She was the type of woman who was either not nearly enough or far too much and often both at the same time.

Rosemary adored her.

"Come, let's do try to sneak away," Lorraine said, her voice much quieter now. "I can't bear the thought of spending the next hour sipping weak tea and nibbling mediocre biscuits with this lot." After the last notes of the final hymn faded into silence, Father Dawson had announced that refreshments would be served under a marquee set up near the vicarage.

Vera hung back, still scrutinizing every detail of the chapel, including the moldings, flanked by Evelyn and Simon, whose puppy-dog eyes never left Vera's face.

Lorraine linked one arm through Rosemary's and one through Stella's and pulled them towards the exit. Alas, an escape was not to be made, not with Evelyn Woolridge standing by.

"Girls!" Evelyn piped up with a motherly sternness that could reasonably have been considered unnecessary given both Rosemary and Stella were no longer children. "To where might you be running off?"

Lending a bit of comedy to the moment, Simon mirrored Evelyn's hands-on-hips pose and frowning expression, though his gaze darted towards Vera and back again. The boy would make himself dizzy if he kept that up for long.

"Drat," Lorraine whispered. "We've been foiled." Louder, she said, "Don't fret, Evvy, we're not sneaking away. Not anymore, surely."

A laugh bubbled to Rosemary's throat, but truly she was impressed by her mother. For as long as she could remember, Evelyn had bent to Lorraine's will, unequivocally and without question—until recently, when something had changed.

Unsure whether Evelyn had simply decided she'd had enough cow-towing or if Vera marrying Frederick had sparked a new sense of equilibrium between the two, Rosemary only knew she was proud.

It had always bothered Rosemary that a woman as formidable as Evelyn Woolridge, who had no qualms whatsoever about telling her husband what-for or coming down on her children when their actions didn't appeal to her, felt so inferior to her supposed closest friend.

For her part, Lorraine positively adored Evelyn and had never attempted to abuse what power she did have over the woman. Lorraine smiled indulgently—fondly, even—and followed Evelyn out the doors and around to the rear of the church.

There, the slightly tattered and faded marquee sheltered several trestle tables, one of which nearly groaned under the assortment of dishes furnished by the good ladies of the church.

A little ways off, in the center of the quaint cottage garden, stood an arbor half-covered in flowering vines, tiny white buds just beginning to erupt from their stems. In another week or so, it would create the perfect backdrop for an outdoor wedding ceremony.

"It's a good thing you didn't decide to have your

reception out here," Rosemary heard Evelyn mutter under her breath to Vera. "Can you imagine if it rained?" She shivered. "What a disaster."

As if to punctuate the notion as a bad idea, Evelyn called attention to the sharp and incessant barking of a nearby dog. "Simply unimaginable."

Vera nodded, her brow knitting even more tightly together than it had been before, and in that instant, Rosemary realized what it was that had made Vera so crazy about her wedding plans: Evelyn.

The revelation came with a sense of resignation rather than shock. Poor Vera had been Evelyn'd. What was worse—she should have known better.

As the congregation milled around under the protective canopy, Rosemary felt it her duty to rescue the bride-to-be, at least temporarily.

She left Lorraine to Evelyn's tender mercies, and feeling Simon's disappointed gaze on her back, nevertheless pulled her friend to a table on the other side of the marquee.

"It's rather nice having tea out here in the fresh air, isn't it?" one of the older parishioners commented. She was a brick of a woman, one who looked as though she did her own garden work. When she stepped around the side of the table, Rosemary's gaze flicked to her feet, and she couldn't suppress a smile when she noticed the woman wore a pair of rain boots beneath her church dress.

Another replied, "Oh, yes, Lottie, you're absolutely right. Perhaps we could raise some funds to make the marquee a permanent fixture." The woman placed a plate in front of one placid-looking fellow, who grunted a thank you before digging in.

Several of the other ladies standing near her nodded in agreement to the comment—all except one, whose quickly-covered scowl hadn't escaped Rosemary's observation. She shared a smirk with Vera, who had unfurled slightly in Evelyn's absence.

"We'll be lucky to get through tea without it pouring down rain," the scowler said, taking a break from arranging a tray of finger sandwiches to look up at the sky, which did have a grey tint to it but was hardly dark enough to pose an imminent threat.

Here we go again, thought Rosemary. If she had to hear one more word about the bloody weather, she might go certifiably insane. Every day for the past week, Vera had scoured The Times, then quoted the forecast endlessly.

"Cleo Holmes, you worry far too much about the weather and far too little about teaching that hound of yours better manners." the one named Lottie chided. "He's been barking for ten minutes now, and I'll remind you the forecast said the storm isn't rolling in until later tonight or possibly tomorrow morning."

Cleo's nostrils flared, but she didn't say anything further, not even when Lottie reached over with a sly smile and moved the platter of sandwiches back to its original position. Instead, she pursed her lips and came to sit opposite Rosemary, next to another older lady who had yet to strike up a conversation but kept an eagle eye on the group of younger folk seated two tables over.

Rosemary resisted the urge to follow her gaze and instead tuned back into the conversation between Vera and Stella. "—thrilled for the break from Lionel. Of course, I adore him, he's my baby boy after all, but he's so rambunctious, always into some sort of trouble. Being pampered is just what I need right now, and Lorraine, bless her heart, has ensured I shan't lift a finger all week."

"I'll see to it that you won't," Vera promised, her attention finally having been diverted from possible wedding day disasters. "I do feel I should apologize for the state of the household. So many cousins have come to stay, the atmosphere is quite disruptive. Between us, I suspect the aunts seized an opportunity to be rid of their progeny for a week." When it came, Vera's smile seemed forced, but then the moment passed.

Stella grinned in reply. "Believe me, after Lionel, a three-ring circus would feel like a holiday. He'll be here for the wedding, of course, to act as your ring bearer. I'm so thrilled you asked."

Bless *Stella's* heart, Rosemary thought to herself. All she needed was a tiny bit of encouragement, and she could talk one's ear off for hours. Rosemary half-listened, enough to murmur encouragement in the right places and shake her head in dismay at others, enjoying the light breeze and the colorful blooms that swayed against it, perfectly content to allow Vera to entertain Stella for a short while.

Some might find a function such as post-church refreshments mundane, even downright dull, but Rosemary enjoyed observing how people interacted in groups such as this one. One could glean much by simply keeping quiet and listening.

A particular type of person might call it nosiness, but Rosemary felt those people should keep their opinions to themselves.

Two tables over, she got a closer look at the Blackburn cousins and their friend, the vicar's daughter. A few of the young men—who had obviously only stayed behind after church let out as an excuse to ogle the girls—took seats at the table and began a dance of flirtation Rosemary remembered well.

Belle Dawson looked just as lovely up close as she had from across the nave, her inky hair and obsidian eyes striking against peaches and cream skin.

She was older than Rosemary had initially assumed,

and it was then she realized Hyacinth and Delilah had been out of school for a couple of years now. Some quick mental math told her they must have already turned twenty or would do so quite soon.

The thought was a sobering one. Rosemary didn't feel much older than twenty herself; it hadn't been so long ago, had it? But the girls looked so young, their cheeks still plump, their brows smooth and unlined.

Furthermore, it was evident that although she and Vera weren't anywhere near over the hill, they had reached the age where the younger ones considered them part of the older crowd. She supposed she couldn't blame them for that, but it still rankled.

"Mrs. Melville, you'll have to let that girl grow up sometime," Cleo said, some of her prickly mood bleeding into her voice.

When Mrs. Melville didn't seem perturbed, Rosemary adjusted her assessment; perhaps this Cleo was *always* persnickety.

"Her father wants to marry her off, you know," Mrs. Melville lowered her voice, but not enough to prevent anyone seated at the table from eavesdropping, "to that Kit fellow who would like nothing more than to push Father Dawson out of the church and take his place if you ask me." No one had.

A glance in that direction confirmed Mrs. Melville's

statement. Father Dawson sat at a table on the other side of the tent, the famous Kit seated next to him. Kit appeared interested in whatever the vicar was saying, yet his gaze occasionally flicked towards Belle with a look of uncertainty.

Finally, Lottie approached the vicar and sat beside him in a way that suggested their relationship was more than platonic. Father Dawson had a girlfriend. The thought surprised and delighted Rosemary.

It did not, however, appear to delight Belle Dawson. If looks could kill, Lottie would have been six feet under. Belle glared at her for a moment, seething, her pretty face contorted into something rather unbecoming.

"Belle!" One of the young men shouted, catching her attention. Her lips turned up in a smile at whatever it was he'd said, and Rosemary almost wondered if she'd imagined the look of hatred on the girl's face.

"He's a handsome enough young man, I must admit," said Mrs. Melville, to which Cleo grimaced and made a disagreeable grunting noise. "Yet, he's almost *too* nice. These girls these days, they all want the dangerous fellow. The one who will certainly break their heart. Kit Weatherford certainly doesn't fit the bill."

Cleo and Mrs. Melville, who by this time Rosemary had gathered was Father Dawson's housekeeper— explaining her intimate knowledge of the vicar's plans for

Belle—exited the table in search of pudding and more tea.

"Rose, are you listening to me?" Stella's question cut through Rosemary's reverie.

"I'm sorry," Rosemary replied, contrite. "What did you say?"

"I asked how things are going between you and Max." Vera, seated on the other side of Stella, waggled her eyebrows at Rosemary.

Leave it to Stella to ask about her love life at a church function. Rosemary chuckled. "Why don't I tell you all about it later tonight," she promised her sister.

For some reason, she couldn't take her eyes off what was happening two tables over. She knew she had been that young; remembered it vividly, in fact, but she was intrigued watching just the same.

"What is so fascinating?" Vera asked, having somehow exhausted all conversation regarding wedding planning and Stella's morning sickness.

"Don't bother. She's enthralled," Stella answered for her sulkily.

Rosemary tossed her an exasperated look. "I'm just feeling nostalgic, is all. Wasn't it all so much simpler back when we were their age?"

Vera smirked and rolled her eyes skyward. "You can't be serious, Rosie. Nineteen was an absolute rotter. We were lucky enough to be at school, not stuck at home under the thumbs of our parents, and they weren't trying to marry us off to the highest bidder, either. Thank our lucky stars."

"It hardly sounds like Vicar Dawson is auctioning off his daughter," Rosemary chided, lowering her voice in the hopes Vera would follow suit and do the same. She might not be nineteen any longer, but she didn't want a tongue lashing from her mother for being rude at church—or nearly at church, as the case may be—any more than she had back then.

"He seems to dote on her if you ask me," Rosemary replied. Even now, while he conversed with Lottie, Father Dawson's gaze rested on Belle, a look of adoration on his face even Vera couldn't deny.

Despite Lottie's assurance the weather would hold, the sky quickly darkened, and the air turned ripe with moisture.

"As much as it pains me to say it, I believe it's time to call an end to the festivities if we would all like to arrive home in dry clothing." Cleo's triumphant glance at Lottie belied her attempt at humility.

"Quite so, quite so," the vicar said agreeably, then raised his voice to make the announcement.

Amid the flurry of activity that erupted, a young man wearing worn clothing and scuffed shoes awkwardly approached the clergyman.

"I'm sorry to bother you, Father, but you did say to remind you about that book I wanted to borrow."

"Yes, yes! Of course, dear boy. It's in the rectory. You know the way."

"Thank you, Father." As the pair turned to do so, the young man's gaze fell upon Belle. He swallowed hard, nodded to her, and walked quickly away.

"Who knew Fergus could read?" Belle followed the uncharitable remark with a trill of derisive laughter that trailed off when something else caught her attention. Belle nudged Vera's cousin Hyacinth, jerked her chin subtly towards the new point of interest.

Rosemary turned to see a male figure standing in the chapel car park, leaning against a motorbike. He looked older than the girls by a couple of years—but his posture and attitude gave Rosemary to think he hadn't matured enough yet to become a man in the truest sense though she suspected he'd argue the fact. Nevertheless, she could see why the girls found him intriguing.

If going only by his looks, Rosemary judged him as precisely the sort of fellow to whom Mrs. Melville referred—the type to break a young girl's heart. The type, based on Hyacinth's narrow-eyed response to Belle's interested reaction and Delilah's slightly more guarded one—to come between girlfriends.

Lorraine's eyes narrowed immediately, but not in the way Rosemary would have expected. The Lorraine she knew would have drunk the handsome man in, even sauntered over to him and made a move of her own.

Perhaps something had shifted, or maybe there was another man in Lorraine's life. Vera hadn't mentioned anything of the sort, but she'd been so preoccupied lately her mother could have shown up with a trained monkey riding on her shoulder, and Vera wouldn't have batted an eyelash.

"Why don't we all take a ride into the village," Belle suggested to her friends. She turned to Kit and, with a coy tilt of her head, asked, "What do you say?"

Kit's gaze flicked to Vicar Dawson. "Perhaps later?" he said, as if uncertain. "We've some sermon notes and"—

Belle had already rolled her eyes and turned away. "And you can't get away. You can be such a stick in the mud sometimes," she said, refusing to spare him another glance.

It took a few moments for the group to gather their things, and by the time they had, Father Dawson and Kit had retired to the vicarage.

The man took a long pull off his cigarette and then blew out a perfect ring of smoke. Then he got on his bike and kicked it to life, following the car down the drive.

"I doubt the vicar knew the girls were heading out with someone like that," Evelyn commented after the lot had disappeared around the bend.

Lorraine balked. "They're hardly girls, Evelyn."

"They're not much more, either," Evelyn retorted. Rosemary couldn't help but agree with her mother.

Well, she thought to herself, *there's a first time for everything.*

"Oh, they're quite all right, I'm sure," Vera said, shrugging. "Do you know how many times I hopped on the back of"—she stopped abruptly—"never mind, you're absolutely correct. He looks like a heathen. Why don't we all just get on home now."

CHAPTER FIVE

Vera—and Cleo, and Evelyn—hadn't been wrong about the rain, much to Rosemary's annoyance. The sky opened up before they pulled away from the chapel, droplets pelting the windshield like popping corn all the way back to Lorraine's. Rosemary thought of poor Hyacinth's ginger hair; she could practically hear it kinking from across the village.

She wondered how the ruffian on the motorbike was doing in this weather, assuming he might find it difficult to maintain his tough demeanor in the midst of a deluge.

Jessop, the Blackburn estate's ancient butler, waited beneath the overhang at the front entrance. He first helped Lorraine and Vera exit their car, unfurling and handing each woman a black umbrella to shelter from the misty rain.

Instead of waiting for him, Rosemary reached behind her seat for her own umbrella but left her bags in the boot for Jessop to bring inside at his convenience.

Rosemary didn't actually mind having been temporarily banned from Woolridge House—quite the contrary, in fact. She was just as comfortable at Vera's as she was at her family home, perhaps even more so since Lorraine subscribed to a far less rigorous approach to household management than did Evelyn.

She let the staff do their jobs with little interference and seemed not terribly particular about anything sother than that the cook produce meals of the highest standards. Despite her svelte figure, Lorraine loved to eat and to eat well.

It was a great coup to be invited to the Blackburn estate. Lorraine was, among many things, a gracious hostess. Nobody left a Blackburn party having had anything short of a fabulous time. She was an entertainer at heart, after all, and the fact she hadn't appeared on the stage in nearly two decades did nothing to squelch her taste for the dramatic.

It also hadn't squelched the enthusiasm of Pardington's elite, who enjoyed bragging about their proximity to a star who, in their eyes, still shone as brilliantly as ever.

Though she was invited to more parties than anyone in three counties, Lorraine only occasionally accepted, tending to prefer intimate gatherings at her own sprawling estate. In addition to playing hostess, Lorraine also found great pleasure in inviting a handful of guests out of the horde who desired entrance to her inner circle.

While the spurned might, on occasion, whisper that the great lady had passed them over out of spite, Lorraine kept her finger on the pulse of Pardington. Preferring to be the center of any drama at one of her parties, Lorraine ruthlessly culled her guest lists of anyone who might be inclined to create a disruption.

Not even Evelyn escaped such selectiveness. During a minor feud with one of her dearest chums, both women had found themselves excluded from at least one swanky do.

Yes, the lady was glamorous in the extreme and only beginning to wear slightly around the edges. But to Rosemary, she would always be something quite more than that: a great friend and confidant, and one Rosemary dearly missed now that she'd moved away to London.

Surprisingly, Lorraine rarely ventured into the city, and therefore the prospect of a whole week at the Blackburn residence warmed Rosemary's heart. It had been years since she'd had chance to do such a thing, and she intended to make the most of it.

The mist of rain turned to a deluge as Rosemary stepped into the foyer. She turned to shake some of the water from her umbrella, only to have the butler remove it gently from her grasp. "I'll just take care of this, shall

I?"

"Thank you, Jessop." The man moved like smoke, she thought, and had the uncanny ability to know where he was needed before he'd been summoned. However light on his feet he might be, when a scampering gang of the younger cousins threaded through the foyer at a run, he nearly lost his footing.

"Here, now, you rapscallions. Have a care!" Lorraine said, without severity, to their retreating backs.

"Yes, Auntie." Came the laughing reply, but the girls did reduce their pace to a more sedate one.

Vera hadn't been wrong when she said her mother's house was crawling with Blackburn cousins. Just the girls; Rosemary wondered if the boys had been jealous watching as their sisters packed their valises and then realized they'd probably been quite thrilled to avoid all the feminine frills.

"Rosemary, you're to bunk in the room adjacent to Vera's this week. I thought the bride deserved some privacy, but of course, you're more than welcome to share," Lorraine explained when all the wet coats had been tucked into the cupboard beneath the stairs and the umbrellas with them.

"I've put all you young ladies in the west wing; the rest of us who need our beauty sleep"—she would never refer to herself as an *old* lady, certainly—"will remain in the east wing, where we won't be disturbed by any late-night activities in which you might choose to indulge." Lorraine gave an exaggerated wink.

Beauty sleep my right foot, thought Rosemary. Lorraine herself most often instigated the late-night capers, and she highly doubted this visit would be any different. One such caper, Rosemary remembered, had involved a midnight croquet tournament on the back lawn.

"Rosie shall stay with me," Vera told her mother. "Let the girls spread out a little more. We don't mind, do we, Rose?"

"Of course not," Rosemary agreed. It might be one of their last chances to engage in the kind of late-night conversations that happen between two lifelong girlfriends. The ending of an era, one might say, and she wouldn't give up spending the last week of Vera's singledom bunked up together sharing secrets.

Abruptly, the storm's waterfall sound ceased, and, out of reflex, it seemed, so did the chattering. Almost everyone standing in the foyer looked up, though what they expected to see besides the ceiling was a mystery.

Vera let out a giggle, and the juggling of luggage resumed.

"I'll gather the candles, my lady," Jessop assured his mistress. "I suspect we're in for a night of it."

"Very good, Jessop, thank you," Lorraine replied.

The rain came and went throughout the rest of the afternoon, some of which Rosemary spent settling in and catching up with her mother and sister.

"Where is the rest of the family?" Rosemary wondered as the raised voices of excited children echoed through the halls. In addition to Hyacinth and Delilah, she'd counted a dozen so far. "Where are all of the mothers? Why aren't the aunts participating in the no-boys-allowed festivities?"

Her mother's eyes darted, for a fraction of a second, towards Lorraine, who was engaged in a lively discussion on the other side of the table. The action piqued Rosemary's curiosity, but Evelyn prevaricated.

"They all live right here in town. It didn't make sense, I suppose, to most of them, to stay on. The children think it's all a great game, however, and in the sunny moments, the horses have been getting the workout they need. You ought to take a ride, dear. It's been ages since I've seen you in a saddle."

Just before dinner, Hyacinth and Delilah returned. Hyacinth wore a bell-shaped cloche in a lovely shade of blue. Probably borrowed from her friend Belle as she hadn't had it with her when they'd all left the church.

"How does my hair look?" Hyacinth said once she'd handed the hat off to Jessop, who carried the dampened felt gingerly between two fingers, taking it to do whatever it is butlers do with wet hats.

Delilah tilted her head to appraise. "Flat on the top, a little puffy at the ends. It could be worse, I suppose."

Huffing out a sigh, Hyacinth brightened as she heard the dinner bell. "Come, Lilah. Let's do change for dinner. I'm simply famished."

At the beginning of the meal, the two girls monopolized the conversation with talk of Belle's impending engagement to Kit.

"One simply cannot understand why Belle would choose to become a vicar's wife," Delilah said as she wrinkled her nose. "Frightful bore of a life if you ask me."

Letting out a ladylike snort, Hyacinth replied, "Nobody did ask you, and why wouldn't Belle want to marry Kit? He's simply lovely. Gentle and kind, and dedicated to the church."

Delilah cocked a brow. "As if those are traits Belle finds laudable in a man. The way they flock around her, she could have her pick of fellows, so why choose to marry an utter wurp?"

Hyacinth had no answer, it seemed, and deliberately changed the subject.

After dinner, Stella followed Rosemary into the room reserved for her and Vera—Vera's old one, though it had been redecorated in gorgeous shades of cream and silvery pink—and sprawled across the bed.

While Rosemary fixed her hair and makeup, Stella asked again how things were going with Max.

Rosemary emerged from the adjacent dressing room, having assumed Stella was listening to her answers, only to discover her sister curled up into a ball, fast asleep. She smiled, shook her head, and tucked the coverlet around Stella, then tiptoed out the door and down the stairs.

Music wafted from the ground floor sitting room, the noise coming from what appeared to be a makeshift dance parlor. All around the room, hips swayed to the beat. Evelyn tapped her toe in time to the music, making Rosemary wonder how many times the crystal wine glass in her hand had been refilled already.

Rosemary found herself standing near the drinks cart and watching while, surrounded by several adolescent cousins gushing exaggeratedly over everything from her dress to her earrings, Vera held court.

Only one young woman, this one older than the rest, seemed utterly uninterested. She broke away from the group and poured herself a healthy dose of brandy, clinking the snifter loudly against the glass as she did so.

"Can always count on Aunt Lorraine to have the best booze, can we not?" the cousin drawled, rolling her eyes and nodding in their hostess's direction. Rosemary couldn't remember this one's name, but she was the oldest of the lot, and her face conjured the sound of a mewing cat.

"Certainly," Rosemary murmured in agreement to the statement but not the tone in which it was delivered.

The cousin licked her lips, first one side and then the other, and Rosemary suddenly remembered: her name was Katherine, but had always gone by the name Kitty, to the delight of the rest of the brood.

Vera, in particular, had enjoyed teasing the girl at every opportunity, which likely explained Kitty's lackluster attitude and the daggers shooting from her eyes straight through Vera's pretty head. And probably also why she hadn't been invited to participate in the ceremony.

"I suppose you're over the moon about this match?" Kitty continued, slurring her s's. "You and Vera being so much like sisters and all. You never did leave any room for the rest of us." She laughed a bitter little laugh and added, "Not that I care overmuch given Vera's status in the family."

The comment caused Rosemary to start and stare at the girl with renewed interest—and a heaping dose of incredulity. Her mouth hung open for a moment while she worked up a smart retort and then thought better of it. Causing a scene in the middle of Lorraine's sitting room certainly wouldn't do.

Virtuously, Rosemary downed her drink and rose to her feet but felt her resolve crumble. Leaning in close so only Kitty could hear her, she murmured, "You'd be surprised to the extent Vera cares about her family—even the ones who may not deserve it."

Kitty attempted a scowl, huffed, and opened her mouth to sputter, but Rosemary held her off with a narrow-eyed glare. "Have another drink, Kitty," she said before sauntering across the room and slinging her arm through Vera's.

Rosemary remembered, now, how Kitty's attitude had always been the proverbial runner in the silk stocking of an otherwise enjoyable weekend.

"This song is far too slow. Let's change it," she suggested now, pulling Vera along towards the phonograph. When she lifted the needle, it was as though she'd pressed a button.

All at once, three things happened. The electricity cut out, a deafening thunderclap sounded from above the manor, and a flash of lightning illuminated the expanse of rolling garden outside the enormous picture window.

Delilah, who happened to have been gazing in that direction, let out a noise somewhere between a gasp and a squeak and leaned forward, pressing her hands against the window.

"Oh! What?" she cried.

"Are you all right, Delilah?" Vera asked into the darkness.

"I—I don't know," Delilah replied. "I think I saw something out the window, but it can't be."

Another flash of lightning lit the garden for a second time, and a few moments later, the electric lights flickered back on. Hyacinth cast a fulminating look at her cousin.

"You're always seeing things, Lilah. I'm sure it's only your imagination," She pressed her forehead against the glass and cupped her hands around her temples to get a better look.

"It's not my imagination. I saw a dark figure of someone lurking around the house. We'll be murdered in our beds." Delilah's squeak made the hairs on the back of Rosemary's neck rise to attention.

Could Black have followed her to Pardington? Rosemary's heart hammered against her breastbone. All the bravado in the world would not save her now. Andrew's voice, still remembered with great clarity, pulled her back from the edge of panic.

The element of surprise only works on the unsuspecting, Rosie.

Rosemary scanned the room for something to use as a weapon, her mind running through the layout of the house to determine what entrance a mass murderer might choose if he thought to take his prey by surprise.

Everyone jumped when the doorbell rang.

So too, had Jessop heard the chime of the bell and come running. He reached the foyer a few seconds before Vera and Rosemary did, but not in time to beat Delilah to the handle. She flung open the door and was nearly crushed by the sopping form of Belle Dawson, who practically fell through the threshold.

"Whatever are you doing out walking about on an evening like this?" Delilah demanded. "And without even an umbrella. You'll catch your death."

"She may still," Jessop commented. "I'll go fetch a warm blanket. Why don't you show Miss Dawson to the downstairs loo?"

"We'll take her into the parlor, Jessop," Vera disagreed firmly. "The upholstery be damned."

Jessop nodded once, spun on his heel, and scurried off in the other direction, making little effort to hide his disapproval, likely of the language Vera used as much as the content of her statement. Rosemary made a mental note to give Wadsworth a raise when she returned to London and then turned her attention to the dripping girl.

"Whatever were you thinking?" Vera scolded. "Prowling around in the dark and in such foul weather. Honestly."

Belle looked a fright with her cap of dark hair plastered to her head, her eyes reddened, and her cheeks paled to porcelain white.

"My apologies," the bedraggled waif spoke to Vera through chattering teeth. "It's t—terribly rude of me to d-d-disturb you with no notice, but I—I didn't know where else to go, and I knew Lilah and Hy were here. I d-do hope it's not too big an imposition."

"Not at all," Vera replied. "We've plenty of room, and you've disturbed nothing. We were just about to head to bed, weren't we, ladies?" she said pointedly, dismissing everyone who wasn't part of the wedding party and earning herself more than one disappointed pout in return.

"Now, let's get you warmed up." Vera escorted Belle into the parlor, plunked her down on a settee facing the fireplace, and stoked the coals until the temperature rose a few degrees.

Setting the brass poker back on its holder, she brushed her palms together and then straightened her skirt before turning kind eyes back to Belle, whose teeth had finally stopped chattering.

"Would you like a ride back down to the vicarage?" Vera asked gently. "Or would you prefer to stay here and ride back with us in the morning? I'd planned to take a look at the sanctuary once more anyway. You'll have to bunk up with one of the girls as we're quite crowded."

"I'd hate to be an imposition if you've already a full house," Belle said, making a move as if to stand.

"Nonsense, the more, the merrier."

"You'll stay with me. Delilah talks in her sleep," Hyacinth insisted. She threw a look in Delilah's direction, daring her to contradict. "Come, you need dry clothing. I'm sure I have something that will fit you."

"Thank you, I'm ever so grateful." Belle looked nothing of the sort as she allowed her friends to lead her upstairs.

CHAPTER SIX

Delilah and Hyacinth entered the dining room late the following morning with a sheepish Belle Dawson in tow. All evidence, save a bit of redness around her eyes, of the previous evening's excitement was gone, and she had taken great pains to ensure every hair was in place.

Her eyes flicked momentarily to Vera, who treated her to a bright smile, before settling somewhat nervously on Lorraine.

"Mrs. Blackburn," she said, quite politely, "Apologies for my intrusion last night. I do hope I did not put you out."

"Nonsense, dear," Lorraine replied easily. "It's no trouble at all. Any friend of the girls' is always most welcome." She lavished her nieces with an indulgent smile, and Rosemary cocked an internal brow, having noticed not one of them returned it with a proportional level of enthusiasm.

"I do hope you didn't catch a draft," Lorraine pressed

gently. "What on earth were you doing out in the middle of the night?"

Lorraine Blackburn was able to ask such questions without coming off as a busybody, although that's precisely what she was.

"Oh, just taking a walk," her composure regained, Belle explained with a wave of her hand.

"In the rain?" Lorraine asked, quizzical.

Belle smiled serenely. "It wasn't raining when I left," was all she said by way of explanation, and then she dug into her breakfast with gusto.

"And your father?" Lorraine prodded. "I assume you rang to inform him of your whereabouts. Parents do worry, you know." She spared a glance at Vera. "No matter how fully grown their children might be."

"I haven't, no." Belle quailed under Lorraine's steady gaze and then excused herself to go and place the call.

"He hasn't answered," she said when she returned.

"Probably out scouring the countryside for his missing daughter." Lorraine put on an expression stern enough to rival Evelyn at her worst.

"I'll just run along and let father know I'm quite all right." Belle laid her napkin alongside her plate. Her appetite seemed to have flown.

"I'll go with you," Delilah offered.

"We'll all go," Vera decided. "I'd like another look at

the chapel."

Outside, the sun shone brightly, and a chorus of chirping birds rent the air. "Doesn't the warm breeze feel just lovely?" Rosemary asked Vera, raising her face to the sky. "Perhaps we ought to walk down?"

Vera nodded in agreement and turned to her young cousins. "What do you say, girls?"

Hyacinth nodded to indicate she thought the idea an acceptable one, but when Delilah grimaced, Hyacinth's expression shifted to match.

Delilah held up a kitten-heeled foot, "These are far too pretty to cover in mud. Besides, if it starts to rain again, we'll all be forced to spend the evening taking turns ironing out Hyacinth's hair." She smirked at her cousin, causing Hy's freckled cheeks to pink and her shoulders to droop. "Let's drive instead."

"If Vera wants to walk, we should walk," Belle argued, earning herself an eye roll from Delilah.

Busy eying Hyacinth's chin-length bob with concern, Vera shook her head. "It's quite all right. Lilah makes a good point. It looks like rain, still."

Belle shrugged and obediently piled into the back seat with her friends while Rosemary climbed into the passenger side. She thought it likely would have taken less time to walk, even considering the mud, given the number of potholes they were forced to navigate around during the short trip down the drive but made no protest.

Instead, she half-listened to the conversation between the three young ladies, her thoughts wandering down a meandering path of their own. How long ago it seemed—though it wasn't, really—that she was a girl of just barely eighteen, trying to decide what she wanted to do with her life.

There had been a boy then, too, who caught her fancy. She might have had a happy marriage with him; a gaggle of children; a manor down the lane from Woolridge House; a regular seat in the second pew every Sunday morning.

It was Vera who'd talked her out of it. Vera, who'd pointed out that she hadn't seen more than a square inch of the world and that she'd plenty of time to be a 'boring old flat tire.'

She'd not uttered a word of protest, however, when, not so very long after, Rosemary had announced her intention to marry Andrew Lillywhite. But of course, Andrew had been different than any man she'd ever met before.

Vera's soft spot for Rosemary's late husband had only endeared her further in Rosemary's estimation—a remarkable feat considering the depth and breadth of her affection for her oldest friend. Tears sprung, unexpectedly, to her eyes as it occurred to her how difficult it must have been for Vera to navigate her own grief while carrying Rosemary through hers.

What was it about weddings that made one so very nostalgic?

She dabbed her eyes, smiled indulgently at Vera's profile, and returned her attention to the conversation ricocheting around the backseat.

All three of the younger set were in high spirits as they exited the car and tripped up the church steps ahead of Rosemary and Vera, who followed at a more sedate pace. Inside, their footsteps clickety-clacked against the wood floor as Belle led the way down the aisle towards the sanctuary.

"Papa," she called out, receiving no reply save the echo of her own voice. "He must be at home," she said with a shrug, continuing down the aisle and leading the ladies through a door at the back of the church.

They continued, a duck-like row of spring hats bobbing their way up the short lane leading to the vicarage.

Belle disappeared inside and returned a moment later with a quizzical expression on her face. "He's not here. I can't imagine where he's gone off to. Mrs. Melville hasn't arrived yet, but his bed's been made. Perhaps he became distracted on his morning stroll. It certainly wouldn't be the first occasion. Vera, you're more than welcome to look around inside the church while I hunt him down."

She turned in the direction of the garden, calling out once more, and something—a feeling of dread—convinced Rosemary that Belle oughtn't to be left to search alone. "Wait," she said quietly to Vera, stopping her from returning to the church.

Vera nodded once, and they hurried to catch up. Rosemary heard Belle's gasp and the quickening of her steps before she could see what had caused the exclamation, the dread turning to acid in her stomach even before Belle cried out.

"Papa!" Her voice was etched with concern, but only a touch of fear, yet Delilah and Hyacinth had stopped dead in their tracks, forcing Rosemary and Vera to press past them to get a view of the prone figure lying beneath the arbor in the center of the garden.

Rosemary could tell there was nothing to be done before she reached Father Dawson's body. She'd seen enough dead ones to recognize the signs.

"Belle, no!" she cried, too late.

Belle crouched down next to her father and tried to rouse him. His head lolling to one side and exposed cloudy, unseeing eyes and angry-looking, mottled bruises around his neck. "No!" she screeched, the pain and the horror of it now turning her voice into something truly excruciating to hear. "Papa!"

Hyacinth doubled over and ran for the hedges, where

she promptly deposited her breakfast while Delilah's face froze into an expression of shock and sorrow. She quickly recovered and helped Rosemary and Vera pull Belle off the ground and lead her, sobbing, into the vicarage.

Rosemary immediately rang the police while Vera set about brewing a pot of tea and left Belle in the sitting room flanked by her girlfriends.

"Yes, Father Dawson," Rosemary answered the constable's questions. "He appears to have been strangled, but of course, that will require confirmation," she said, taking care to keep her voice low and spare poor Belle any more pain. "Come quickly, please. His daughter is in a right state, and we won't want any of the parishioners to happen by the churchyard and find him lying there. Yes, thank you."

"They'll be right along," she explained to Vera. "It isn't as though there's a murder in Pardington every day."

Vera snorted bitterly, "No, not every day. Just the days when you and I are in town. Please remind me why I decided to have my wedding here and not in London?"

"We find dead bodies in London, too," Rosemary reminded her. "But why don't we worry about your wedding plans once we've dealt with this one, shall we?"

At least possessing the good sense to appear chagrined, Vera nodded. "You're right. That came off as rather insensitive. It's a terrible tragedy, and I feel just terrible for that poor girl." She peered around the edge of the doorway and assessed Belle's appearance. "She's distraught."

"As she well ought to be. It was quite a shock, and that's not even the beginning of it."

The sound of the front door opening interrupted Rosemary's train of thought. "Good afternoon, Father," she heard a sing-song voice waft down the hall and recognized that of Mrs. Melville. "I'm terribly sorry I'm late, but there was a downed tree blocking the street, and I had to go round the other way.

It was Mrs. Melville, the cheeriness of her voice in such stark contrast to the reality of the day it made Rosemary's stomach turn. She came round into the sitting room, her eyes still on a piece of post she must have rescued from the box, and then stopped short when she looked up to notice the expression on Belle's face.

"Whatever is the matter, child?" she said, rushing over to Belle and taking the girl's hands in hers.

Instead of answering, Belle dissolved into a puddle of tears.

"Belle, dear," Mrs. Melville implored once more before turning her attention on Rosemary and Vera. "You're Lorraine Blackburn's daughter. I remember you from church yesterday. What are you doing here? Where is Father Dawson, and what is wrong with Belle?"

Luckily, neither Rosemary nor Vera was forced to answer the question outright as the gravelly crunch of a car pulling into the drive sounded from outside. "You'd better come with us," Rosemary said to Mrs. Melville, whose eyes darkened in reply.

She followed without another word save for a muffled squeak prompted by the sight of the police car parked outside the vicarage gate.

"Someone called in a report of a dead body," the constable, an impossibly skinny boy with acne scars covering his cheeks, appeared skeptical, but before his inquiry could be confirmed, Mrs. Melville let out a gasp.

"A dead body!" she squeaked, looking back and forth between the officer and Rosemary.

"I'm sorry to say, it's Father Dawson," Rosemary explained.

Mrs. Melville, in direct opposition to Rosemary's expectation, closed her mouth with a snap and went completely silent. Her eyes welled with tears, and after a moment, she tried to speak, but no sound escaped her lips, and the conversation moved on without her.

"Out back, in the garden, Inspector…what is your name?" Rosemary asked, vehemently wishing they'd sent a grown-up officer instead of one who more closely resembled a schoolboy.

"That would be Deputy Brown," a smooth male voice

laced with condescension emitted from the car as a distinguished-looking—and handsome, Rosemary couldn't help but notice—man unfolded himself from the passenger seat.

"I'm the inspector. Inspector Trousseau of Scotland Yard," he said boastfully, taking Rosemary's hand and lingering for a moment longer than necessary. "It's a pleasure."

Whether he meant it was a pleasure to meet her or that it ought to be considered one for her to have met him, she couldn't be sure, but something told her it could go either way.

Rosemary's stomach jerked, and she wiped her hand on her dress, hoping to erase the trace of his touch, then turned to Mrs. Melville. "Why don't you let Vera take you inside where you can keep an eye on Belle. She could use a gentle, motherly hand right now. I suspect you are the closest thing to one she's got."

The comment seemed to rouse Mrs. Melville, and she appeared grateful to have been dismissed. She nodded her head at Rosemary and then Inspector Trousseau and disappeared inside the cottage, leaving Rosemary to explain how the body had been discovered.

"We'd pulled up in front of the church. The black car there belongs to Lorraine Blackburn, who lives just up the hill." Rosemary explained the relationship between Vera,

Delilah, and Hyacinth, as well as the circumstances of how the lot of them had come to be traipsing through the churchyard that morning.

Sick with sorrow over the unnecessary death, Rosemary strode quickly towards the garden and Father Dawson's body, the young constable and Inspector Trousseau trailing behind.

She felt Trousseau's gaze like a weight upon her back, and wished it were Max with whom she walked towards tragedy. The comfort of his presence would be most welcome.

CHAPTER SEVEN

"There." Rosemary flinched at the way her voice disturbed the hush of death. She pointed, quite unnecessarily, when the body came into view. "It looks as though he's been strangled with something resembling a belt, or maybe a sash of some kind. The mussed dressing gown could indicate a struggle, or perhaps the rain and wind are responsible. Regardless, it wouldn't have taken much to overpower Father Dawson, particularly given the slightness of his build."

The young constable stared at Rosemary for a moment, his mouth hanging open in a way that made her nostrils flare at the unspoken insinuation that a woman had nothing but fluff between her ears and therefore could not evaluate a crime scene.

On the other hand, Inspector Trousseau appeared impressed, slightly bemused, and more than a little intrigued.

"An aspiring lady detective we have, do we?" he

chortled, the handsome becoming less so with each passing moment.

"I see no reason for such a term to exist," Rosemary snapped uncharacteristically. "After all, you didn't introduce yourself to me as 'Male Inspector Trousseau,' did you?" Something about the man made her feel edgy and confrontational.

"Regardless," she continued while his eyes widened in surprise and before he could formulate a retort, "If you examine Father Dawson's dressing gown, you'll find it's soaked through, which given the weather indicates he exited the vicarage and was killed last night after he'd changed for bed, rather than this morning. Additionally, we found the body before the maid arrived, and Miss Dawson, the vicar's daughter, says his bed hadn't been slept in."

Deputy Brown snorted. "Got it all figured out, do you?" He asked rhetorically and then proceeded to mumble something along the lines of, "Ought to let the professionals do their jobs."

Rosemary pierced him with a glare but didn't sink to his level by responding. The inspector gathered his wits and said, "Brown, go get my kit out of the car. And take your time. Apologies, Miss Lillywhite," he added when the constable had hurried off to do his bidding.

"It's *Mrs.* Lillywhite," she corrected automatically.

"Again, apologies," Inspector Trousseau said, dipping his head down in an awkward motion that resembled a bow or the tipping of a hat. Her eyes narrowed to slits when he added, "Your husband is a lucky man to have a wife like you."

Rosemary's lips pressed into a thin line. "Perhaps he was, but he's no longer with us. Just like Father Dawson." She held her palm in the poor, dead vicar's direction and raised one eyebrow.

"Yes, yes, of course." The inspector cleared his throat, shook his head as if to clear it, and knelt down by the body. "You're right," he said, making what seemed like a concerted effort to keep from sounding surprised.

"I would estimate this man died yesterday evening; cause of death: suspected strangulation. We'll need the coroner for a more accurate estimate, but that was an astute observation on your part."

Why was it every time Rosemary found a body she was forced to deal with some inspector insinuating she didn't know her elbow from a hole in the ground?

She supposed she ought to be asking why she kept finding bodies so very often in the first place, but since it didn't appear she was going to stop being in the wrong place at the wrong time, she decided not to bother.

"Thank you," she said instead, woodenly. "Am I clear to go inside and find my friend? There are three young ladies in there who have had quite a fright."

"Of course, of course," the inspector said, waving a hand. "Not everyone is as calm and collected as you are in the face of tragedy." There was a question in the tone of his voice; he'd like to understand why she hadn't gone to pieces, and she only hoped he wouldn't decide to make her his next suspect. How awkward might that be?

She didn't really want to explain herself, not to him.

"There's the doctor now," she said instead of answering. A long black car had pulled into the drive, and Rosemary rushed back into the vicarage with a mind to ensure poor Belle wasn't forced to watch her father be loaded into the back of it.

Inside, Mrs. Melville sat on the sofa next to the girl, her back ramrod straight and a distant look in her eyes as though she were still in shock. Which, Rosemary realized, she probably was. Tears streamed silently down Belle's face, leaving saltwater tracks that trailed all the way to her neck.

Vera and the Blackburn cousins had retired to the small kitchen adjacent to the sitting room, and Vera now poked her head into the doorway and motioned for Rosemary to join them.

"We thought some privacy was in order," she explained, and Rosemary noted both Delilah and Hyacinth appeared relieved to have escaped the uncomfortable situation. "Neither Belle nor Mrs. Melville seemed to notice we'd left, so I suppose it didn't make much difference."

After what seemed an interminably long wait but was probably no more than ten minutes, Inspector Trousseau knocked on the front door and then entered without waiting for admittance. Under the circumstances, his disregard for the polite niceties was entirely forgivable, as much as Rosemary would have liked to use such behavior as another point against him.

"Miss Dawson?" He glanced briefly at Delilah and Hyacinth, who had poked their heads out of the kitchen door but then turned his attention to the sofa. He seemed to recognize the grief on Belle's face as that belonging to a daughter who has just lost her father, and there was no denying he seemed pained by the sight of it.

Belle looked up at him, bewildered.

"I'm afraid I need to ask you some questions about your father," Trousseau continued. "Beginning with, when was the last time you saw him alive?"

The word 'alive' used in that context pained Belle so deeply a wince knitted her brow together and caused her fingers to clench around Mrs. Melville's hand. The action roused the housekeeper, who shook her head and emerged from her dazed state.

"You don't have to answer that, Belle dear. You don't

have to answer any of his questions." She patted the girl's hair while glaring at the inspector with an expression of hatred.

"Let her be; she's lost enough for one lifetime, first her mother and now her father as well. She needs time to recover. As do we all."

Inspector Trousseau's cheek twitched once. "I appreciate what Miss Dawson is facing, certainly. But her father has, it appears, met his end at the hands of another. Murdered, that is to say."

As if there had been any doubt of his meaning prior to the clarification.

"My priority is figuring out by whom. Therefore I am obliged to take Miss Dawson's statement while the details are still fresh in her mind."

"Oh, pish posh! There is nothing poor Belle can tell you that will help you solve the case. She doesn't have any more idea of what happened than you do."

Mrs. Melville's eyes widened and then narrowed.

"Is that what you're getting at? That she might be involved, somehow? She's just a child. An innocent child."

Now, the inspector's cheek twitched several times in quick succession, and his complexion ruddied.

"Mrs. Melville, with all due respect, Miss Dawson is of legal age to answer my questions, and furthermore, she's under obligation to do so. As are you, I might add. I'd be rather curious to know your whereabouts yesterday evening."

Mrs. Melville's nose lifted in the air, but before she could wind up another sharp remark, Rosemary stepped in. "Could I speak with you?" she asked Trousseau loudly.

In response, she received a lengthy stare that ended in an annoyed sigh. "This is highly irregular," the inspector grumbled but followed Rosemary into the kitchen.

Before she had a chance to berate him, Hyacinth stepped forward. Her face had gone so pale the smattering of freckles across her nose and cheeks stood out boldly.

"Belle could not have hurt her father," she said with calm determination. "I know because she was with me last night. With all of us, really, but we shared a room, and I know she didn't leave."

"You know she didn't leave," Trousseau repeated Hyacinth's statement in a mocking tone.

Rosemary interjected. "Wouldn't it be all right for you to return tomorrow to question the girl? Perhaps some of the shock will have worn off, and she'll be able to tell you what you need to know. Unless you seriously believe Miss Dawson killed her father and is mere moments away from a confession?"

Something about that conclusion simply didn't add up,

in Rosemary's opinion, though she did suppose anything was possible. Somehow, she suspected she'd have better luck getting Belle Dawson to tell her all her secrets than Inspector Trousseau would have done, but she wisely kept that thought to herself.

He seemed to consider the question. "Did you not say the girl arrived late last night, soaking wet and distraught? Doesn't that scenario resemble the proverbial 'smoking gun'? I'd like the *lady detective's* opinion." All pretense of politeness evaporated as quickly as drops of water on a hot rock.

Rosemary felt the urge to kick Inspector Trousseau squarely in the shins, or perhaps a location slightly higher, and she resisted, but just barely.

"One never counts out even the most unlikely of suspects, Inspector. Even lady detectives know that much. I'm merely stating the obvious—you can't get blood out of a stone, and that poor girl hasn't spoken since she discovered her father's body."

"Fine," Trousseau finally acquiesced. "I'll give Miss Dawson until tomorrow to come forth with her statement, but if she doesn't cooperate, I'm afraid I'm going to have to open an investigation into her relationship with the deceased. The same goes for Mrs. Melville."

With that final warning, Trousseau finally took his leave, to which all of the ladies left at the vicarage agreed was well overdue.

Nobody, not even Rosemary, knew what was the polite thing to do; should they leave or should they stay and try to help Belle and Mrs. Melville in some way? The foursome consulted and ultimately decided they ought to stick around at least long enough to make certain there was a decent meal in the house.

When the doorbell rang, Rosemary abandoned the task to Hyacinth and Delilah, urging Vera to follow her along to the foyer. Upon learning the identity of the person on the other side, both vehemently wished they'd opted to return to the Blackburn estate when they'd had the chance.

Kit Weatherford looked confused when the door opened, and two unfamiliar women stepped out. "Uh, hullo? I'm here to see the vicar," he said, a question in his voice as if he wasn't sure anymore exactly what it was he'd come there to do.

Upon hearing of the tragic death, Kit's face drained of color, and his eyes filled with unshed tears. He wiped them quickly away with the back of his shirt cuff and swallowed hard. "I can't—no," he said, trembling. "Belle, where is she? Is she all right? Does she know?"

"She's inside, but she isn't speaking with anyone. Perhaps she'll talk with you, however," Rosemary suggested, holding open the door to allow him entry.

Belle would him now more than ever.

"Belle," he cried, rushing to kneel in front of her and take her hands in his. Rosemary felt a little sorry for him when Belle didn't respond and decided she might have to recant her earlier supposition. "Belle, I'm so sorry," Kit repeated.

He tried for a few more minutes, but when she didn't glance in his direction or acknowledged his presence in any way, Kit stood up and collected himself.

"I suppose I ought to take my leave," he managed to say, his voice choked with emotion.

After Rosemary and Vera watched him leave and walk down the path back to the church, they decided they no longer cared about proper etiquette, gathered the girls, and piled back into the car.

CHAPTER EIGHT

In sharp contrast to the drive down that morning, the ride back up to the Blackburn estate felt positively funereal. Nobody spoke a word save for one comment from Hyacinth. Halfway up the drive, she sighed and said, "Poor, poor, Belle," in a voice so filled with sympathy and sorrow it rendered any reply quite inadequate.

Of course, news had yet to travel to the Blackburn estate, and life there carried on as normal, though somewhat more hectic than usual given the seemingly never-ending wedding preparations.

At the moment, the household had gathered for tea in the dining room. Everyone sat almost literally in the same place they'd been that morning, making it seem even more so that the events that transpired in between meals had been a terrible nightmare.

"Oh, Evelyn, dear, you know I adore you, but you can't possibly be serious?" Lorraine drawled as Vera and Rosemary crossed the threshold with Hyacinth and

Delilah in tow. She sat at the head of the table where she could preside over the family, her hair tied up in a midnight blue satin turban. She was staring at Rosemary's mother as though Evelyn had grown a second head.

"Lorraine, darling," Evelyn replied in the sickly sweet voice she used when she was placating a child. A child. or someone she considered to be acting like one, which she clearly did of her dearest friend at this particular moment. "You do recall it's something old, something new, something borrowed, something blue, and *a sixpence in her shoe*, do you not?"

Lorraine geared up to retort but, seeing the expressions on her nieces' faces, abandoned the conversation. "What is it? What's happened?"

"I can't listen to you say it," Hyacinth cried. "It's all just—just too awful!" She strode quickly back out of the dining room, and Rosemary could hear her footsteps mingle with her sobs as she ran across the foyer and up the stairs.

"Someone ought to go with her," Delilah sighed. "And it probably ought to be me. Why don't I bring the girls upstairs as well?" she said, taking charge. "None of them need to hear the sordid details."

"What sordid details?" Evelyn squeaked, her already thin patience having entirely evaporated.

Vera held up a hand and waited while Delilah gathered

up the younger girls, leaving only Kitty, who was on the edge of her seat with curiosity, behind.

When the girls were out of earshot, Vera sank into a chair and explained, "Father Dawson is dead. Murdered, by the looks of it, wouldn't you say, Rosie? You are the expert, after all."

"I'm hardly an expert, but in this instance, I'd hardly need to be," she said, following suit and taking a seat next to Vera. "He was strangled, no doubt about it, with something resembling a belt of some sort."

Evelyn gasped, her hand fluttering to her throat, and Lorraine let out a bitter expletive. "Such a lovely man, whoever could have wanted to hurt him?"

"That's always the question, isn't it?" Rosemary asked, a bitter edge to her words. "And the answer is that someone isn't who they seem to be—either the victim or the murderer, and more often than not, it turns out to be both."

Kitty turned to Rosemary with a sharp look. "You won't find any skeletons in Father Dawson's cupboard. He was a good, kind man who wouldn't hurt a fly. I've seen him capture spiders and return them to the garden. Whoever did this to him is nothing short of pure evil, inside and out."

"I'm sorry I didn't know him as well as you. He seemed rather a pleasant man indeed when Frederick and I met with him to request he allow us to be married in the parish," Vera mused sadly. "As neither of us resides in Pardington at the moment, it was within his purview to say no, but he couldn't have been more agreeable."

"Yes, well, doesn't that just top his list of good deeds?" Kitty snapped sarcastically, causing Vera's—and everyone else at the table's—head to whip in her direction.

Vera's eyes narrowed. "What exactly is that supposed to mean, Kitty?" She demanded.

"Not a thing in the world, Vera." Kitty's voice had turned sickly-sweet. "Simply that if asked, I'd have guessed it would take a full five minutes before you twisted the conversation from Father Dawson's death to your all-important wedding festivities. I would have been wrong, wasn't I? As it only took you one."

Lorraine, seeing the crestfallen expression etched across her daughter's face, stood from her place at the head of the table. "Katherine Blackburn, I realize you're grieving, and so I'm going to afford you a small amount of latitude. You've never been one to pull punches, and ordinarily, I consider that quality to be admired—but not when it's at someone else's expense."

"Particularly not at Vera's expense. Understood." Kitty nodded once, curtly, at her aunt, rose from her chair, and then stalked out of the dining room without another word.

Evelyn reached over and patted Lorraine's arm comfortingly. "These young ladies today don't know what they're saying. Neither of our girls," she smiled indulgently at Rosemary and Vera, "would have ever dared speak to us like that, nor Stella either."

Lorraine returned the statement with a thin smile. "Our girls are quite something, aren't they?"

The two 'girls' in question exchanged a look that might have been a smirk under other, less macabre circumstances, meant to convey their surprise at how the tables had now turned in their favor.

It seemed spending an extended amount of time with the young ladies of the family had made their mothers remember to be thankful their own daughters had long since passed through the awkward years.

"I didn't mean it like that," Vera whispered, her face crestfallen. "I'm not a monster. What happened to Father Dawson is terrible. He seemed a kindly old fellow to me, and I was happy to have him perform the ceremony."

Rosemary reached over and patted Vera's hand. "Nobody thinks you feel anything other than sorrowful. Kitty is just angry. She's always had a fiery temper. She'll cool off eventually."

Fiery temper was a nice way of saying Kitty was a brat through-and-through, and everyone at the table knew it.

"The fact remains," Evelyn spoke up, "that you and my

Frederick are to be married in a matter of days. Insensitive or not, we've no intention of allowing this unfortunate turn of events to disrupt our plans any further than necessary. Do we, Lorraine?" Evelyn took a casual sip of her tea and peered at her friend as if she'd merely asked if Lorraine wanted jam on her toast.

Vera's eyes nearly popped out of her head. "You aren't suggesting we press forward with plans to get married at the church after what happened?"

"Whyever not?" Evelyn asked, appearing positively mystified.

"I don't think Vera wants to get married fifty feet away from where we tripped over a dead body," Rosemary explained to her mother, exasperated.

Evelyn brushed aside the concern. "Pish posh. Don't you know there have been more dead bodies in that church than live ones?" The statement had the opposite effect than intended, and Vera blanched.

"Whether or not I'm willing to be married, there is hardly the question," Vera said, exasperated. "Who's to perform the ceremony if not Father Dawson? And furthermore, won't it be in rather poor taste to continue on with our plans as though nothing has happened? It seems to me the best course of action is to move the entire event back to London. I'm sure, Mother, we could get one of the smaller rooms at the Savoy even on exceedingly short notice."

The suggestion—and a resulting current of animosity—hung in the air, and for a moment, it appeared as though one of Vera and Evelyn's epic arguments was ready to commence. Before the fragile peace snapped completely, Lorraine stood and banged her fist on the table loud enough to rattle the silver.

"You will *not* be getting married in London, Vera." It was as sharp a tone as Rosemary had ever heard mother take with daughter, the only other instance having occurred when she'd caught five-year-old Vera trying to trim Rosemary's bangs with a nail scissor. "Even if we *could* arrange for another venue, the banns have already been read. You're getting married in Pardington because the only other alternative is to postpone, and that's not an option."

Vera sank back in her chair and avoided Lorraine's gaze like a sullen child. Instead, she narrowed her eyes at Rosemary and sulked, "I never should have let you talk me out of eloping. This is what I get for trying to make everyone else happy. Doesn't anyone care about *my* happiness?"

"Vera Blackburn," Lorraine said tersely, her eyes flashing. It had been the second time she'd had to resort to her stern Mother voice, and doing so wasn't something she relished. Before Lorraine could unleash her fury, the sound of the telephone jingling from the other room cut through the tension.

"Miss Vera," Jessop intoned, "It's Mr. Woolridge for you."

With a resigned glance at Rosemary, Vera left the table and hurried out to the hall. Her muffled explanation to Frederick could be heard in the silence she'd left behind.

After a few seconds, Vera's voice rose another octave or two, and Rosemary could clearly hear her telling Frederick not to panic. Another handful of moments was all Evelyn could take. She sighed, threw down her napkin, and followed after Vera.

Evidently, she'd divested Vera of the telephone because a moment later, Evelyn said, "Frederick, darling, it's your mother."

Who else might it be? Rosemary wondered with a roll of her eyes.

"We're all perfectly safe here, and you're not to come up and interfere. It's been a long day. These girls just want to have a nice cuppa and then sink into a hot bath. Let them be, and you may come by tomorrow to do your doting. Frederick," Evelyn's voice turned hard, and whatever her son said as a result seemed to placate her.

"All right then, it's settled. We shall see you tomorrow. And tell your father he will be expected to answer for himself as well. Missing church, I tell you the nerve of the lot of you!"

The conversation ended quickly after that—no doubt Frederick rushed off the telephone, realizing he was indeed on the end of a losing battle. And now his future wife had his mother on her side? Well, tomorrow would do just as nicely after all.

CHAPTER NINE

"Now," Evelyn said, clapping her hands on her way back into the dining room. "I believe that's all settled, isn't it, Vera?" The question was purely rhetorical, and anyway, there was no time for a response because Evelyn kept right on talking. "You and Frederick will be married at the church, as planned."

Vera shot a panicked look at her mother and then, finding no purchase there, turned to Rosemary with a plea in her eye.

"I'm sorry you're upset, Vera darling," Lorraine interjected. "But quite a number of people have gone out of their way to assist in the planning and execution of this wedding, not to mention the many guests who will be arriving from out of town. There's hardly time to alert them all of a major venue change, so it's simply out of the question."

Rosemary had never seen Lorraine be so adamant about something that seemed so reasonable. Vera certainly had a right to feel uneasy about being married so close to where Father Dawson died.

This change in Lorraine gave Rosemary pause to wonder for the second time within half an hour, what was the source of the palpable tension she'd felt since arriving at the Blackburn estate.

"We're still missing a vicar, Mother," Rosemary said without much conviction. One or the other was one thing but put Evelyn and Lorraine on the same side, and nobody else stood a chance. "Who will perform the ceremony?"

Evelyn waved a hand and sighed as if her daughter were daft. "It's not for me to say, but I assume the parish priest would be the one to take over Father Dawson's duties."

There wasn't much for Vera to say, though Rosemary knew keeping quiet was taking a tremendous toll. She finally broke, but there was no fight left in her.

"You two can arrange the whole thing. Just tell me when to arrive at the church. Since you don't need my input, I believe I'll retire to my room. Rose, you're also retiring."

Rosemary did as she'd been commanded, with one last disapproving look thrown over her shoulder. She needn't have bothered. Her mother and Lorraine had already returned to their planning, their heads bent together conspiratorially.

"That woman is positively infuriating!" Vera exclaimed when Rosemary had securely closed the door, and she'd flopped down onto her bed.

"Which one?" Rosemary asked wryly.

Vera hesitated for only half a heartbeat. "Both of them."

"Would it make you feel any better if Father Dawson's murderer were caught?"

The answer was a decided no if the darkening of Vera's already thunderous eyes were any indication. "If I say no, I'm worse than the monster Kitty thinks I am. Of course, I want his killer found, but please, Rosie, stay out of this one. For me, I'm begging you."

"I've no intention of becoming involved. Inspector Trousseau is more than qualified and perfectly capable of solving this crime." The only problem was, Rosemary was already in the middle of it—something she seemed to have a talent for—and though she meant what she said, that didn't mean trouble wouldn't come looking for *her*.

"I mean it, Rose," Vera pressed, having recognized the look of uncertainty on her friend's face. "We agreed not to run off and elope for *you*, and if you leave me to the wolves—and by that, I *do* mean Delilah and Hyacinth—I will *never* forgive you."

It took a bit more reassurance before Vera let Rosemary off the hook and a healthy dose of brandy from the dressing room snifter before she fell into an exhausted sleep. Rosemary covered her with a blanket, brushed the hair away from her forehead, and closed the door softly behind her before taking a deep, cleansing breath.

The feeling of peace lasted all of five seconds when she heard the sounds of a furtive conversation going on two doors down in the library.

"What do you suppose she'll do now?" Hyacinth asked, sad but resigned, her voice steadier than Rosemary would have imagined given her outburst in the dining room just a couple of hours prior.

Delilah replied sharply, "How should I know, Hy? If that inspector has anything to say about it, she'll see the gallows. What she ought to do is hire a solicitor, though where she'd get the money for something like that, I couldn't say."

Rosemary realized Delilah and Hyacinth were talking about Belle, and she tiptoed a little closer to the door to hear better.

"One of Aunt Lorraine's baubles would cover the whole expense," Hyacinth said with a trace of bitterness. "But surely Belle doesn't need a solicitor, you don't think?"

Delilah said, "I don't think she killed her father if that's what you're asking. She doesn't have the capacity for murder in her. But whether she needs a solicitor is another matter altogether."

Exasperated, Hyacinth snapped, "I wasn't asking if you thought she killed him, Lilah. I was asking if you think the *police* will think so."

A sneeze gathered behind Rosemary's eyes, and she squeezed them shut against it. She couldn't walk away now. Her curiosity had been piqued.

"I certainly hope not. I don't fancy being forced to answer all of that wretched inspector's questions, and neither should you."

Hyacinth let out a squeak. "Why would I need to answer questions?"

Delilah huffed, "Seriously, Hy, sometimes you really are daft. Belle was here with us, so she couldn't have been at the vicarage murdering her father. You opened your big mouth and vouched for her. Are you positive she didn't leave in the middle of the night?"

There was silence for a fraction of a second, and then Hyacinth said, "Of course. You know what a light sleeper I am; I'd have known if Belle got out of bed, and I'm positive she didn't."

Something akin to guilt colored Hyacinth's voice. "Besides, I brewed her a cup of lavender tea, double strong. She slept through the night, trust me."

"You drugged our friend?" Delilah asked, sounding more impressed than disgusted.

Hyacinth balked, "I didn't *drug* her, I gave her a good night's rest, and we both know she needed it. She was so worked up over"—

Finally, Rosemary couldn't hold it back any longer, and the sneeze escaped, revealing her position outside the library door and abruptly ending the conversation.

Quickly, she stepped around the corner as though she'd innocently been on her way down the hall and hadn't heard a thing.

"Oh, hello girls, I didn't realize anyone was in here," Rosemary lied. "Have you seen a pair of reading glasses? I think I left mine on the side table yesterday evening."

Both Hyacinth and Delilah shook their heads, but the way Delilah's lip turned up at one corner made Rosemary think she hadn't been as convincing as she thought.

Luckily, she was saved from making further excuses by the arrival of a disheveled Stella. She wandered into the library with her eyes half closed, her hair standing on end and a crease mark across her cheek.

"I thought I heard your voice, Rosie," Stella said through a yawn. "What time is it? I'm starved."

Rosemary took her sister's arm and led her back out the door grateful for the opportunity for escape. "It's past dinnertime, Stella dear, but I'm sure we can scrounge up something delectable. Why don't we go brush your hair, Miss Sleepyhead?"

Chapter Ten

Rosemary woke before dawn the next morning and settled into a favored spot in the solarium. One that faced the Blackburn estate's rear garden while the sun crested the hill behind a thin cover of clouds.

Wisps of white and grey swirled in the distance as if uncertain whether they fancied turning into a full-on storm or merely enjoyed driving Vera mad with worry.

Under cover of night, Rosemary had tiptoed into the kitchen like an unwelcome bandit and fixed herself a pot of tea. She'd even, with some small amount of clandestine pleasure, nipped a blueberry scone from beneath the glass-domed platter resting so enticingly on the sideboard.

Unfortunately, she had yet to bring herself to do much more than push it around her plate.

All she could think about was Father Dawson's murder and the conversation she'd overheard the previous evening. What had Hyacinth been on the cusp of revealing? What had Belle been so worked up over? Did it have to do with her father's death? Rosemary doubted it very much but her curious nature wouldn't be quelled so easily.

The problem was, she'd promised Vera she'd stay out of the investigation; leave it to the police to solve. As off-putting as Rosemary may have found him, Inspector Trousseau did seem fully capable of accomplishing the task.

On the subject of tasks, there would hardly be time to complete the myriad of ones she'd valiantly offered to take off the bride's hands—and certainly not enough to investigate a murder while doing so.

Indeed, she wanted to see justice done for the vicar, but even more so did she desire to ensure Vera and Frederick's wedding went off without a hitch.

Her cheeks pinked with shame even thinking such a thought—for, of course, justice was more important than what, ultimately, amounted to a frivolous party. May her tongue rot and fall out if she should ever repeat that opinion in front of Vera.

After all, extravagant weddings were a luxury reserved for the wealthy and surely, must ultimately have little bearing on marriage quality. In fact, some might argue that the most modest affairs yielded the most successful unions. Except, Rosemary didn't care.

She adored Vera and, despite her constant ribbing, thought the sun rose and set on her brother. The two of them declaring their intent to spend the rest of their lives together—adjacent to Rosemary, of course—made her stomach churn with excitement, relief, and a thousand other emotions she couldn't begin to name.

She knew Vera would do her best to tell the story of her wedding—minus just a few details—and that nobody listening to the tale would suspect the event had been anything short of perfectly lovely. Nobody, that is, except her best friend and matron of honor.

Rosemary would know that the sparkle in Vera's eye was a little dimmer than it ought to have been, that the smile on her face could have stretched a little bit wider, and that the joy in her heart was just the tiniest bit diminished.

No matter what Rosemary did—even if she decided to get involved, and even if she could solve the case in record time—it wouldn't bring back Father Dawson. It wouldn't make things right. Ferreting out the truth never did, and as much as she wanted one less murderer roaming the streets, she wished to make Vera happy more.

It was the best wedding gift she could give her oldest friend, and Rosemary made her mind up then and there to throw herself full force into the wedding plans and let

Inspector Trousseau do his job.

With an effort, she drew her mind back to the present and took a few bites of the coveted scone. She suspected she would need her strength for whatever lay ahead. Unable to pin down Kit Weatherford, Evelyn had secured another vicar, Father Davies, from Pardington's sister parish, solving the most immediate problem with ease.

That it hadn't taken more than two telephone calls was enough to inflate Evelyn's head even more than usual, but since Rosemary suspected there would be at least one more crisis before the wedding bells were scheduled to ring, she decided to let her mother take the win.

Before she actually heard a stirring from the upper floors, Rosemary felt the household's gears begin to squeak and slowly grind to life. Now, the estate was filled with daughters and cousins, but soon Lorraine would be alone again, in this drafty old place.

Quite like how it will be when I return to London. The sudden thought took Rosemary by surprise. While she longed to have her peaceful home back, she fully expected the emptiness to carry a resounding echo when compared with the life and laughter Frederick and Vera wore like a mantle wherever they went.

The arrival of a carload of men hailing from Woolridge House provided a welcome interruption from worry. Even from the very rear of the estate, Rosemary could hear the sounds of an engine roaring up the drive. She guessed, correctly, that it was Freddie at the wheel.

Rosemary gathered her skirt and hurried into the foyer where she met Vera, whose furrowed brow and red-rimmed eyes indicated she hadn't slept any more soundly than Rosemary had.

Indeed, Frederick emerged from the driver's seat, not bothering to close the door behind him as he caught sight of his fiancee.

"How are you, my love?" Frederick asked, checking Vera over as if finding a dead body might have left a visible mark.

Rosemary rolled her eyes and approached Max, who exhibited concern for her welfare but in an appropriate amount.

"You must have the worst luck of anyone I've ever met, Rose," Max said into her hair as he leaned in and deposited a kiss on her forehead. It was a tender gesture, no less endearing or heart-swelling than Vera and Frederick's display, merely a touch more restrained.

She smiled thinly. "Yes, I think you might be right."

"I'm not taking you anywhere ever again," he replied lightly, an attempt to shake her doldrums.

It went some way, and she cracked a genuine smile. "You're *my* date, remember? It's you who's become entangled in my unfortunate luck."

"I suppose it's a good thing I'm a Chief Inspector and therefore used to such atrocities as murder." Max seemed to hear the words as they left his mouth, and his brow crinkled together. "From a certain perspective, of course."

"Too bloody right," Frederick piped up, having overheard the last part of the conversation. "Any man who dates Rosie is going to need one strong stomach."

Rosemary resisted the urge to swat her brother but was saved the trouble when Vera did the job for her. "Don't be such a...what did the girls call it?" Vera paused to think. "Oh yes, try not to be such a wurp, my dear."

"Where's Father?" Rosemary asked, peeking into the back seat of the car and finding it empty.

Frederick glanced at Max and shifted uncomfortably from one foot to the other. "He didn't think it wise to leave the younger cousins unattended."

It wasn't like Frederick to be so succinct.

"Are you certain he's not hiding from Mother?" Rosemary countered.

"No, Rosie, I'm not certain," Frederick fired back. "Just between us, he's let the household get in a right state in Mother's absence."

"Explain," Rosemary ordered.

"The cook came down sick on Saturday. On Sunday, the housekeeper declared us all heathens, announced she, too, was ill and took to her bed. You'll forgive me if I'm not keen on stumbling headfirst into the lion's den. Let's just focus on the disaster at hand, and we'll let Father worry about Father."

She held her hands up in surrender, "All right, have it your way. We've enough to concern ourselves with as it is." Rosemary entertained little doubt the men had earned the bout of household mutiny.

"Yes," Frederick murmured, "It's quite unfortunate what happened to Father Dawson. I always did rather like the old chap. What I knew of him, in any case."

"Seems everyone did," Rosemary replied, "except someone who obviously hated him enough to murder him."

Frederick shrugged. "It's a problem for the police, isn't it? Or are you planning on doing a little sleuthing on your own?"

"She will do no such thing," Vera spoke with great vehemence. "I have forbidden her from diving headlong into danger when there's enough of it swirling around her head already."

While he might enjoy a reputation for indulging in certain vices, Frederick had not the control over his face needed to become good at gambling. Even now, his features betrayed his reaction to the news.

"And she fell in with your plans just like that?" Frederick snapped his fingers.

"Not as such," Vera admitted. "But in the end, I managed to win her over to my side."

"Under pain of threat." Rosemary glowered but put no real heat behind the response.

Another rumbling sounded from the direction of the road, and Rosemary gazed down to the end of the drive. Her heart sank at the sight of the official-looking vehicle. When Inspector Trousseau stepped out of the driver's seat, it plummeted to the floor.

"Mrs. Lillywhite," he said, emphasis on *Mrs.*, and tipped his hat in Rosemary's direction.

Max's brows lowered, and Frederick turned a narrow eye on the newcomer.

"I didn't expect we'd meet again so soon," the inspector continued, his tone silky smooth and mildly suggestive.

As if out of reflex, Max's arm went round Rosemary's back to settle possessively on her waist. Inspector Trousseau's gaze followed it, and he bristled visibly for a split second before immediately relaxing back into his cool demeanor.

"I don't believe we've met. Inspector Charles Trousseau, at your service." He held his hand first to Frederick and then to Max as though he were an afterthought.

"*Chief Inspector* Maximilian Whittington, at *your*

service," Max retorted, just as smoothly.

Vera leaned in and whispered a scandalous comment in Rosemary's ear, "Give them another minute, and they'll pull out their Billy Clubs to see which one is bigger."

Chapter Eleven

Lorraine broke the tension when she poked her head out of the front door. "My dears, you must come inside. Your mother wants to know what you're doing out here"— she stopped short, getting a good look at Inspector Trousseau.

"Well, and who might you be?" Lorraine straightened, thrusting her bosom into view and batting her eyelashes.

Rosemary counted that as one question answered. Her lifestyle might have undergone a slight change, but the old Lorraine was still in there somewhere.

Inspector Trousseau repeated his introductions, his own chest puffed up to match hers. Rosemary and Vera shared a look of amusement, though it didn't last long under Max's annoyed gaze.

"Trousseau, is it? What a delightful coincidence."

Trousseau frowned.

"We're in the midst of wedding preparations." When he frowned again, Lorraine waved her hand in a delicate manner. "Never mind. Do come in. We've breakfast laid out in the dining room."

Always an attentive hostess, Lorraine linked arms with the inspector as though they were the dearest of friends and led him across the foyer.

He seemed to have, at least for the moment, forgotten about Rosemary, and for that, she was relieved.

"What brings you by this morning?" Lorraine asked when she'd tucked Inspector Trousseau into a spot near the head of the table and motioned for the maid to fill him a plate.

Hyacinth and Delilah exchanged uneasy glances at the sight of the inspector, though he hardly spared one for either of them until after Lorraine's question had hung in the air for a long moment.

"I'm here on business, unfortunately," he finally admitted.

Kitty, seated across from the inspector, chewed slowly and watched him with avid interest.

"Naturally, we've heard all about poor Father Dawson," she said, her brow furrowed in a sympathetic expression. "Have you any news? Has the killer been found?"

"Not as such." Jaw clenched, the inspector bit the words off short. However handsome of face he might be, his manner reflected a rather boorish nature. "I have spoken to the lady of the house next door to the vicarage—a Mrs. Holmes—and learned that the reverend had a paramour."

Trousseau's gaze flicked between the three girls until Lorraine called his attention with a pointed remark. "Yes, he had been squiring Lottie Lewis of late. I quite thought they made a lovely couple and hoped they might decide to marry. A vicar, I always say, needs a good wife with solid moral standing to provide the feminine touch for parishioners."

"Be that as it may," Trousseau sounded impatient. "Ms. Lewis confirms she arrived by car just before dark, whereupon she was greeted by a snide remark from the vicar's daughter."

Hyacinth and Delilah gasped in unison while Kitty merely sat and waited for the next revelation. Inspector Trousseau noted each reaction.

"According to Ms. Lewis," he finally continued, "Miss Dawson left the premises while Ms. Lewis went inside and then traded words with the vicar over his daughter's utter lack of good manners. Tempers flared, and she left in a huff, only to return some time later, at which point she heard a motorbike pull up near the graveyard. I've been informed there's only one young man hereabouts who drives a motorbike, a lad named Alistair Cox. Mrs. Lewis then heard the youth speaking with a young woman and is willing to swear the young woman in question was none other than Belle Dawson."

Eyes round as saucers in a face gone pale, Hyacinth swallowed hard. "Belle never mentioned," she broke off with a start as if someone—presumably Delilah—had kicked her under the table.

Trousseau paused to see if Hyacinth would elaborate, but she'd clamped her mouth shut and tipped her head down to stare at the table.

"Would you care to explain how Miss Dawson was asleep in this house at the same time she was also engaged in conversation with a young man some half a mile away?"

Lorraine flicked a glance at Hyacinth, who continued to remain mute.

"This property is one of only two bordering the churchyard, and some of your…"

"Nieces," Lorraine supplied.

"Some of your nieces are on intimate terms with the victim's daughter. It's to be expected I would have a few questions, particularly given that you all are, collectively, Belle Dawson's alibi. Not a very good one, I might add."

Evelyn audibly gasped, but when Lorraine's eyebrow didn't even quiver, Rosemary knew she *had* been expecting as much.

"Evelyn, he's merely doing his job," Lorraine said,

glancing once at her friend and then reverting her gaze back to the inspector. "He certainly can't believe these girls had anything to do with the vicar's death. That would be absolutely ludicrous!"

There was a warning to her tone, and though she kept the serene smile pasted across her face, Lorraine's eyes flashed with motherly love.

Oblivious to the danger he faced, Trousseau treaded into deeper water. "Can't count anything out. It wouldn't be professional, now would it?"

Rosemary had heard the spiel before; she'd been married to a former officer turned private investigator and was now dating a chief inspector. She tuned Trousseau out and instead watched the effect he had on the others seated at the table.

Red of face, and her eyes stormy, Evelyn looked like she might burst, but the notion of her speaking up was laughable. Not rocking the boat was Evelyn's specialty. Even given her recent willingness to go toe-to-toe with Lorraine, Rosemary knew better than to expect her mother to argue with a police officer.

Frederick concentrated on the plate of kidneys in front of him, making Rosemary wonder what the Woolridge men had been eating since the cook's sudden illness. She shuddered to think.

It certainly looked as though her brother hadn't eaten

at all the way he shoveled it in, and it only took another moment for it to dawn on her that Frederick always followed a night of too much drink with a day of too much food. She rolled her eyes and let them fall on Max.

He was listening with rapt attention, unusually quiet. His eyes flicked to Rosemary, and they were hard—hard and black. A shiver went down her spine.

She'd never seen Max look at her like that before, even when he'd been angry, which was, admittedly, a rare occasion and usually predicated by her having done something rash and dangerous.

What she could have done to set him off this time, Rosemary didn't know for certain, but it didn't take a detective to figure out it probably had something to do with Inspector Trousseau.

"This is a big house," Trousseau was saying when Rosemary tuned back in. "Anyone could have stolen in or out after dark. We'll need to take statements from everyone who was on premises last night."

"I'll give you mine right now," Kitty spoke in a tone rife with bored indifference. "As the company failed to interest me, and there was nothing better to do, I went to bed with a book. But you're free to check my windowsill for signs of passage."

Lorraine, who had remained relatively calm until

now, looked as though she would like to commit an act of crime against her niece and then another against the inspector.

"Has Alistair Cox corroborated Lottie's statement?" This from Hyacinth in a tone so hushed Rosemary had to lean in to hear when the inspector bade Hyacinth repeat her question.

The inspector's mouth snapped shut for a moment before he answered. "No, he has not, as I have been unable to run him to ground. Quite suspicious, don't you think?"

"I can't see why." Unable to stop herself, Rosemary offered an opinion she might have been better keeping to herself. "What possible motive would he have?"

He contemplated the question for a moment, and then shrugged. "That's what I aim to find out. The man is said to be well off, or to at least look the part. Appearances often deceive. However, there are other motives than money. Off the top of my head, it could be Mr. Cox whispered his confession in the wrong ear and then had to do something drastic."

"But I digress. That is conjecture, and I prefer to work with facts. For now, let's concern ourselves with the other side of the equation," Trousseau said, rising from his chair and brushing his toast crumbs on the floor. "How many entrances to the house, and where are they located?"

"Jessop," Lorraine spoke more sharply to the butler than her usual tone, a sign of agitation. "Would you kindly show the inspector around?"

She nodded to where Jessop stood, hands clasped, awaiting orders.

"I shall, of course," Jessop answered the unasked question, his eyes on his mistress. "However, I believe the inspector will find that he needs only to concern himself with the one at the front."

"And why might that be?" Trousseau's brows lifted at what he probably considered an insouciant response.

"You see, sir," Jessop's face gave nothing away. "The side door near the servant's quarters has been blocked by wedding frippery for nigh on two weeks now, and the recent spate of weather has caused the garden door to swell. None of the young ladies would be able to get it open as I am unable to do so myself."

Jessop schooled his features into a polite mask and studiously avoided looking towards the door in question.

"To my knowledge, the house was locked up tight and remained that way from the time Miss Dawson arrived until quite early the following morning."

Trousseau's face lit up. "Precisely as I suspected. *To your knowledge.* I'm sorry, Mr. Jessop, but I can't allow you to speak for the entire household."

Lorraine opened her mouth to say something as a representative of the entire household but, to Rosemary's disappointment, never got the chance because Max intervened.

"Inspector Trousseau is merely trying to do his job," Max explained, making deliberate eye contact with his hostess. "Perhaps it would be best to let him inspect the grounds."

"Quite right. Father Dawson was outside in his pyjamas in the rain. It's unlikely he was lured into the garden by a stranger. Yours is one of a handful of homes in proximity to the scene of the crime, and everyone here knew the vicar in some capacity."

Max turned to Lorraine. "Let him look around, and then he can be on his way. I trust the inspector," and now Max leveled him with a gaze, "will handle himself expeditiously and with the utmost respect.

"Assuredly, assuredly," Trousseau said, his tone deliberately mild. The look he threw at Rosemary was anything but, and it set Max's blood on a slow burn.

When he'd gone, Max leveled a look at Rosemary. "The sooner he does his job, the sooner he's out of our lives. I suggest you let him get on with it."

"I wouldn't dream of doing otherwise. There is, after all, a wedding in the offing, and Vera has asked me to refrain from sleuthing until it has gone off without a hitch," Rosemary delivered in the same even tone Max had used and took some small delight in the way his jaw clenched.

CHAPTER TWELVE

Rosemary followed Vera around the village of Pardington the next afternoon, her arms laden with shopping bags, a blister beginning to form at her heel. Why anyone needed six pairs of hose for one day, she couldn't begin to fathom, especially considering under Vera's floor-length gown nobody, save Frederick, would have any reason to see her legs.

Of course, she'd kept that thought to herself while Vera chose several nearly identical pairs in sheer white and then moved on to the nudes.

Next came gloves, and those took another hour despite the presence of at least two perfectly good pairs in a box at home. When Vera began to second guess her lingerie choices, Rosemary put her foot down.

"Vera, my dear, you may be running on some sort of bride's petrol, but I'm on fumes," she said when they'd stopped at the car to stash the bags in the boot. "I need a strong cuppa and an enormous scone."

It looked as though Vera might argue, but she took a deep breath and nodded. "All right. I suppose I've cleaned out the Pardington shops by now—oh no!" Vera stopped short and ducked behind the boot, dragging Rosemary with her.

"What on earth are you thinking? Are you positively mad?" Rosemary demanded, exasperated.

Vera shushed Rosemary's attempts to ascertain why she was being manhandled, peered around the side of the car, and then quickly slammed the boot.

She shoved an arm through Rosemary's elbow and then swiftly pulled her towards Shropshire's Tearoom, where they tumbled inside in a heap.

Vera peered through the front window, looking furtively back and forth, and then finally relaxed her shoulders. "Thank goodness, he hasn't spotted us. I cannot bear to spend the next hour being badgered with questions by your cousin Simon."

She held up a hand against Rosemary's protests. "I know you adore him, and that's lovely for you, but you would feel differently were it your skirts he chose to sniff around."

"You could do worse," Rosemary said with a mock straight face. "He *is* the heir to Mother's family fortune, you know." She nodded sagely until Vera's ears turned red and then burst out laughing.

"It's good to see age hasn't stolen your senses of humor," came a scratchy old voice both Rosemary and Vera knew well.

They both whirled and caught sight of Mrs. Shropshire, the proprietor of the tearoom, staring at them with her head cocked, a wicked smile on her lips.

"Mrs. S!" Rosemary cried, striding towards the old woman and allowing herself to be embraced and kissed on both cheeks. Vera took her turn as well, and each received a thorough judging.

"Too thin by half and far too beautiful. You've obviously been smiling too much. Sooner or later, you'll have laugh lines all over your forehead, and then it's just a hop and a skip until your decolletage resembles crepe paper the day after a birthday party."

Mrs. Shropshire had an odd sense of humor. One never knew what scandalous comment might fly out of her mouth, and that was, in fact, the quality of hers both Rosemary and Vera found most endearing.

Moreover, the dear lady's lack of pretension reflected her utter disdain for the bounds of society, which she most often showed with her penchant for attending the occasional fete wearing trousers in place of ladylike attire.

"Tell me you do plan to attend the wedding, Mrs. S," Vera begged now. "You did receive the invitation, did you not?"

Beaming, she nodded. "Of course, dear, I wouldn't miss it for the world. You and Freddie," she turned to Rosemary then, and with wide eyes and a sarcastic tone, said, "who would have guessed it? You foolish children. I'm thrilled you've finally accepted one another. I predict you'll have a long and prosperous marriage."

Vera grinned, basking in the glow of Mrs. Shropshire's praise. She would have begun waxing on about the ceremony and her dress if she hadn't noticed the atmosphere in the room buzzing at an abnormal level.

"What's all this about?" Vera asked, gesturing.

"You're like a bloodhound, child, except you've a nose for gossip. This particular bit only just came over the wire in the last half hour. Lottie Lewis has been questioned as a suspect in the vicar's murder!"

"Oh, my!" Vera replied, surprised. Rosemary hadn't seen it coming either but chose not to vocalize her opinion. Inspector Trousseau hadn't indicated anything of the sort during yesterday's visit, but perhaps he'd kept that card close to his belt.

Lottie and the vicar had appeared quite happy when she'd seen them together following Sunday service. Something about it just didn't feel right. Then again, what went on behind closed doors...

"How did you find out?" Rosemary wanted to know.

Mrs. Shropshire leaned closer across the table. "That's just it—I got it direct from Mrs. Melville from over at the church. On her way back from picking up the vicar's nicest suit from the tailor, she stopped in, nearly full to bursting with the news. By the time she'd left, the whole tearoom knew every detail, and it's all anybody's been able to talk about since."

"Tell us every detail!" Vera said, her wedding plans forgotten for the moment.

Rosemary elbowed her in the ribs. "You made me promise to stay out of it, and now you're going to stick your nose in?"

"There's a difference between being involved and being informed, Rosie. Now, hush and let Mrs. Shropshire reveal the salacious details! I, for one, could use the distraction."

That was all the prompting she needed, and Mrs. Shropshire launched into a retelling of Mrs. Melville's tale.

"Evidently, the inspector came by the vicarage early this morning, insisting he take Belle's statement. Mrs. Melville tried to put him off, of course—she treats that young lady like her own, though she's no claim, and half the time Belle is simply rotten to her, but I suppose you can't fault a girl for that during a time like this."

Mrs. Shropshire's recounting meandered into

conjecture and her own opinion so frequently telling event from speculation turned into a chore, but nobody listening could say they'd been less than thoroughly entertained. Rosemary sifted through the mishmash more easily than most.

"The inspector insisted, and according to Mrs. Melville, she and he engaged in a standoff right there on the vicarage front stoop—until, that is, Belle came to the door and broke it up. She told the inspector the last time she saw her father was when she left the vicarage just as Lottie Lewis came to call. Belle denies having had words with Lottie at all; claims she said hullo, went on her way, and didn't return the rest of the night."

Rosemary knew Belle was telling the truth on one count. She'd been at the Blackburn estate that night, amongst several witnesses. However, she didn't buy for one second that the girl hadn't mouthed off to Lottie Lewis.

The rest of Mrs. Shropshire's story ran along the same lines as Trousseau's recitation of facts. Lottie had returned to the vicarage, heard Belle and Alistair together. "They say criminals always return to the scene of the crime, and since no one else has come forward, it seems the inspector has sussed out the time of death. Lottie was the last to speak with him, which automatically makes her a suspect."

Mrs. Shropshire sat back, her hands spread as if that explained it all. Given what she knew from having examined the scene herself, Rosemary wasn't so sure.

"Pure conjecture, is it not?" She pointed out. "Father Dawson's body lay in the garden all night, during intermittent rain and fluctuating temperatures. The time of death is approximate at best. What other evidence is there against Lottie? Did they find the murder weapon?"

"Not as such. The inspector found a pair of mud-covered Wellies in her coat cupboard," Mrs. Shropshire said with a shrug. "Hardly a smoking gun in a provincial village like Pardington. Lottie walks every day, rain or shine. She claims it keeps her feeling youthful, and it certainly keeps her fit. There's no denying that."

Rosemary thoroughly agreed, having noticed Lottie's build during the church social. Unfortunately, she also knew that in provincial villages like Pardington, people gossiped from sunup to sundown and didn't much care if the smoking gun was actually smoking or not.

"She's capable, certainly, but means and opportunity are only two-thirds of the puzzle. What would be her motive?" Vera's eyes narrowed as she also considered the implications. "Money seems unlikely as the vicar wasn't a wealthy man. Revenge? For what? He didn't strike me as capable of physical force, at least not against a woman like Lottie. By all counts, he was a nice, god-fearing man loved by most of Pardington."

Mrs. Shropshire peered at Vera with the eyes of someone much older, wondering how the youth of the day had become so daft. "There are an infinite number of reasons to kill, and oftentimes any number of them at once. People can try one's patience, don't you know, and no matter how meek or mild, everyone has a tipping point."

Vera shrugged. "Maybe so, but the killer being Lottie feels wrong to me."

"I suppose you think Belle did her father in?" Mrs. Shropshire asked, but she looked towards Rosemary for the answer.

From out of the front window, Rosemary watched a small dog go prancing down the street sans owner. She smiled until she caught Mrs. Shropshire looking at her, realized such an expression might be in poor taste.

"We have conflicting versions of the event surrounding the death. If some of the statements are true, others must be lies. Where Belle's accounting of the evening falls on the line between the truth and a lie would be far easier to determine should young Alistair step forward. As he has not done so, Belle remains on the suspect list," Rosemary said and then winced as Vera threw her a look that could burn metal to slag. "If I were investigating, of course, which I'm not."

"But if it wasn't Lottie, what are the odds of another person skulking round the vicarage on a dark and stormy night?"

As it turned out, there had been at least one more person "skulking round the vicarage" the night of Father Dawson's death, a fact that was proved less than a day later when, through the gossip chain delivered news that Fergus Poole—having heard about the content of Belle's statement, no doubt—came forward to explain he'd also seen the vicar and Lottie together the evening of the vicar's death.

Not only had he seen them together in the vicarage, but he'd also overheard them arguing rather loudly. When pressed with regards to what the argument had been about, Fergus declined to comment.

Given the source, not to mention the timing, Rosemary viewed the information with a healthy pinch of skepticism. Fergus hadn't come forward until after Belle made her statement, a statement that meant little in and of itself. Lottie being the last one to see the vicar alive didn't automatically make her his murderer.

Fergus's evidence, however, *was* incriminating. Now, two individuals had pointed the finger at Lottie, the second story corroborating the first. She doubted Inspector Trousseau had any idea that Fergus pined for Belle, but it was clear as day in Rosemary's mind.

How far Fergus might go for her, well, that was something Rosemary could only guess. In some twisted way, she hoped they were both telling the truth, and Lottie really had killed the vicar. The inspector could wrap up the investigation, and all the unpleasantness would all be done and over with.

It would mean she hadn't been wrong to stick up for Belle. It would mean the niggling concern she'd given the girl too much credit, the flutter in the pit of her stomach that flared whenever she remembered the look of loathing Belle had given Lottie, could finally cease.

As Rosemary stepped out of the teashop, the little white dog raced by her, his brown eyes merry, his body an agile blur of flying fur. Behind him, and far outstripped by his speed, Cleo Holmes huffed and tried her best to keep up.

"Dash, you get back here, you little menace."

Panting and red in the face, she chased him around the next corner, coming no closer to him than she'd been when Rosemary first laid eyes on the little beast.

Chapter Thirteen

"Wealth, health, happiness." Vera plopped exactly five sugared almonds into pretty, tulle-lined boxes, punctuating each with a recitation of the blessing it was meant to bestow. "Longevity, fertility. That last one can wait a tick, however." She added, with a wink and a grin in Rosemary's direction.

That morning, Vera had risen full of energy. The first words out of her mouth had been, "I'm getting married in three days!" and she'd been able to talk of nothing else since. It didn't appear to matter that half of her comments went unanswered, and neither did she seem aware of the sighs that usually followed.

Truth be told, Vera could have been far more obnoxious than she was, and her spirits had improved greatly with each day that separated her from the murder of Father Dawson.

Being treated like a princess and doted on by the household staff also had something to do with her jovial mood, Rosemary felt certain. Vera had only to snap her fingers, and whatever she desired would be delivered on a silver platter—sometimes, literally.

On this particular morning, three days before the wedding, she had gathered the bridesmaids, plus her mother and Evelyn, into the atrium. All the tables and chairs had been set up in preparation for the reception, and some put-upon staff maid had been tasked with arranging the almond favor boxes.

Two hundred of them—one for each reception guest— were now laid out on a long banquet table at one end of the room. Whichever the maid it had been, she ought to have felt grateful for one thing: Vera didn't expect her to fill the boxes.

"It *means* something if we stuff them ourselves," Vera had explained excitedly. "Each box is lined with tulle. The almonds go in; the tulle gets fluffed, and the box gets tied with a bow. Couldn't be simpler. I want nothing more than to know every guest from my wedding is wishing me and Freddie blessings on favors packed with love!"

Rosemary had wanted nothing more than to roll her eyes, but she didn't dare do anything of the sort for fear of pushing Vera too far. The bride's dark side was one sarcastic comment away, and she wasn't a monster anyone wanted unleashed.

So instead, she listened to Vera's instructions and made

it a point to act as though counting out sugared almonds for three hours was precisely the way she wanted to spend the day.

The only one who appeared thrilled by the prospect was Stella, but that was likely due to Jessop's doting. As far as he was concerned, there were two princesses in the house.

He'd dragged an overstuffed armchair in from one of the sitting rooms and carefully elevated Stella's feet with a padded stool. She'd her own tray filled with tea and nibbles and a down pillow for her head, and Rosemary estimated she'd dozed for most of the afternoon.

"Why, Vera, did you say fertility could wait? Do you and Frederick not want children right away?" she asked in one of her rare lucid moments, chewing thoughtfully on an almond.

Vera tried to cover a grimace but wasn't entirely successful. "I adore children. So does Freddie, and of course, we want to have them someday."

"You aren't getting any younger, dear," Lorraine said, plopping a handful of almonds into a web of tulle without bothering to count them at all. Evelyn shot her a stern look, intercepted the box, and removed the extra nuts.

It was then she seemed to register what Lorraine had said, and she looked at her friend in surprise. "I thought you were *far too young*," Evelyn rolled her eyes at the phrase, "to be called Gran."

"Oh, Evvy, don't be such a stickler. I say all sorts of things. Nobody ought to go on believing them all." At that, she tossed a wink in her nieces' direction. For once, both Delilah's and Hyacinth's smiles appeared genuine.

"I'm glad to hear you're behind the subject of children. My Freddie deserves a brood of his own, and now that he is doing the responsible thing and settling down, there is absolutely no reason to wait. No reason at all." Evelyn managed to sound both smug and vehement. Vera took the comment poorly.

"Settling down." Vera sniffed. "Your ever-so-responsible Freddie and the rest of the motley men have managed to drive away both the housekeeper and the cook at Woolridge house."

Evelyn's jaw dropped, and Vera hurried to say, "Only temporarily, I'm sure." She gave her mother-in-law to be a sunny smile.

"You'd be surprised how getting married changes things, Vera," Lorraine had gone on.

"How's that, Mother?" Vera asked wryly, her concentration focused on tying up a tiny box with an even tinier ivory bow. It wasn't the actual doling out of almonds that was tedious. It was the wrapping process. Even Rosemary's dainty hands had cramped.

Lorraine shared a conspiratorial smile with Evelyn and

simply said, "You'll see, dear."

It was nearly enough to make Vera come undone, but Rosemary kicked her under the table to get her attention and then stuck out her tongue like she used to when they were children. The ploy worked, and Vera forgot about the question of procreation, at least for the moment.

"*I* won't see, I'm afraid," Delilah said with no trace of regret or even sadness. "I can't imagine myself *ever* getting married."

Hyacinth stared at Delilah, her mouth hanging open for a moment as though the statement was the most outrageous she'd ever heard. "Why would you think that, Lilah?"

"Because it's true," Delilah insisted. "I possess neither the looks nor the dowry to draw fancy, and it's no secret my personality is considered off-putting. A man doesn't want a wife who will contradict him at every turn, and I don't relish the thought of biting my tongue until the poor sod finally drops dead. Oh, dear, there I go proving my point. That was insensitive given recent events."

Delilah shrugged as though there were little she could do about her chronic case of verbal incontinence.

Hyacinth glowered at her. "Don't say such things, Lilah."

"I already apologized. What more do you want from me?"

"No," Hyacinth said with a shake of her head. "Don't say you'll never get married. It's not true. You're not off-putting, you're just"—she seemed unsure how to actually finish the sentence—"independent."

Delilah smiled indulgently at her cousin, having softened uncharacteristically, and said, "Thank you, Hy, but you needn't fret over my love life—or lack thereof. To be quite honest, I've little desire to find myself entangled."

"Utter nonsense," Hyacinth brushed aside the comment. "Every girl wants to fall in love and get married."

"Oh, dear, sweet Hyacinth, I do hope you get what you want, but don't assume to know my heart," Delilah replied. "Just be absolutely certain you know your own before you make your choice." Now a wicked grin crossed her face. "Throw over too many men, and eventually, you'll run out of proposals to turn down."

Hyacinth's eyes widened. "Lilah," she said pointedly. "That's none of our business, and you shouldn't make jokes."

"What's none of your business?" Vera wanted to know. Up until now, she'd kept quiet, enjoying the banter, but Mrs. Shropshire had been correct in her assessment that Vera could sniff out salacious gossip from fifty paces.

Once she caught the scent, there was no denying her the

satisfaction of extracting every minute detail from whoever had been unfortunate enough to let a tidbit slip.

Whatever this particular tidbit was, it likely had something to do with events Hyacinth and Delilah had been discussing in the library the evening they'd found the vicar's body. Rosemary leaned forward, eager.

Delilah shared a glance with Hyacinth, who shrugged her shoulders and then explained. "Belle decided she didn't want to marry Kit Weatherford after all. She told her father she'd changed her mind, and he kicked up a bit of a fuss. That's why she showed up here the night Vicar Dawson...died. But then, she didn't even want to talk about Kit. She acted as if he no longer existed, didn't she Hy?"

"Yes," Hyacinth said slowly as if wondering if she should say anything at all. She looked around the table, collectively hushed for the moment while the revelation sank in.

So Belle Dawson hadn't been caught out in the rain while on an innocent stroll. Something had happened to change her mind regarding her engagement to Kit, and she'd needed the company of her girlfriends to talk the decision through.

"What a silly girl," Evelyn commented absently. By now, she'd consumed several cups of tea and had pushed the almonds far enough out of her reach it was clear she'd stuffed her last box. "She could have done much worse than that nice boy, and furthermore, her prospects are no longer as bright as they were before her father's unfortunate passing."

"I hate to say it, but you're right," Lorraine replied, shaking her head. "So sad. I still can't believe Lottie Lewis would do such a thing. She always seemed to dote on him. It goes to show you never know what runs through a person's mind. I cannot imagine what that nice man could have done to warrant cold-blooded murder."

Evelyn followed Lorraine's comment with a cluck-cluck noise. "One never does know, does one? Don't count Lottie out so quickly. Whatever the case may be, they'll find the guilty party, or perhaps Rosemary will be the one to work it out."

She said it as though it were an inevitability, and while Rosemary was flattered to know her mother had such faith in her abilities, she wished Evelyn would have kept quiet this once.

"There's nothing to say Father Dawson's actions brought about his death, at least not directly. It might be he learned something in the course of his duties that posed a danger to the killer. In that case, his murderer could have been anyone, Mother," Rosemary said, trying to end the conversation.

"I'm certainly not planning on hanging around

Pardington long enough to question everyone who lives here. Inspector Trousseau knows what he's doing. I'm sure he'll come to the truth in due time." She glanced at Vera and received a grateful nod in response.

"I think it was the housekeeper," Vera chimed in, unable to keep out of it even if she did expect Rosemary to do so. "Mrs. Melville, after all, made it a point to spread the word about Lottie's possible involvement, but maybe that was a cover."

Delilah rolled her eyes. "If Mrs. Melville wanted to murder someone, she'd slip something lethal into their tea. I can hardly imagine her strangling the vicar with her bare hands."

Hyacinth shivered and corrected her cousin. "Inspector Trousseau said the murder weapon was a belt of some kind. It wouldn't have taken someone overly strong. Even so, what reason would Mrs. Melville have to kill Father Dawson? She's out of a job now unless she gets asked to stay on when the next vicar is appointed. Furthermore, she adores Belle, and with the vicar gone, Belle will be forced to leave the vicarage."

"Precisely," Delilah agreed.

Rosemary didn't say a word, but that didn't mean her gears weren't turning. The girls were right. Mrs. Melville did adore Belle—enough to object to the idea of her marrying Kit. Hadn't she said it was the vicar's idea, that he'd been the one who wanted the two together?

Could that be enough to make Mrs. Melville take action? She'd got what she wanted, after all. Belle was no longer getting engaged to Kit. Was that a coincidence, or was it part of what got Vicar Dawson killed?

"Wait, who is the other man who caught Belle's interest?" asked Vera suddenly, after Evelyn and Lorraine had cited the need to rest their aching bones—which likely meant cocktails in the parlor, and everyone knew it.

"How did you come to that conclusion?" Delilah leaned back in her chair and frowned at Vera. "You're absolutely correct, of course, but I don't think we mentioned anything of the sort."

With a graceful flick of her hand, Vera waved the comment away. "Anyone with eyes could see she's a man magnet. There simply *must* be someone else in the picture."

Hyacinth's cheeks pinked, and she said tersely, "Alistair Cox."

Rosemary stared at Delilah in horror. "Oh, no. Not him," she said with a groan. "He's trouble, mark my words. She'll get her heart broken." Rosemary realized she sounded like her mother giving a lecture, and she blanched.

Delilah's smirk returned. "Don't underestimate Belle.

Alistair might be the one who's in for it."

Hyacinth eyed Delilah quizzically. "In for what do you think, exactly?"

"Oh, Hy, really!" Delilah replied, exasperated. "You know nothing at all about men, do you?"

"*Really*, Lilah, for all her playacting, Belle has a great deal of growing up yet to do," Vera scolded as if she had intimate knowledge of Alistair's type, which she very likely did.

Still, Rosemary thought, someone had met Alistair in the graveyard on the night of the vicar's death. Hyacinth said she'd given Belle something to help her sleep—not that Rosemary was supposed to know that secret—so who was the mystery woman? Could Belle have risen while Hyacinth slept?

Despite Jessop's assurances to the contrary, Rosemary knew firsthand that slipping out of the Blackburn house after hours was no difficult feat. She and Vera had managed with great success to sneak out on several occasions. If the butler knew about those late-night forays, he never let on. Nor did Lorraine, so it stood to reason Belle could have managed perfectly well.

Or Alistair's assignation had been with someone else entirely. One more frustrating conundrum in the mystery she'd promised Vera she wouldn't solve.

"These girls have lived sheltered lives. Belle hardly

knows what that kind of man is really like. It would be a pity if she ended up stuck with him, wouldn't it?"

When she returned to the conversation, Vera's point of view struck Rosemary as odd, and she said as much. "You aren't a typical bride, are you, Vera?"

"Whatever do you mean?"

"Well," Rosemary decided she'd already ventured into dangerous waters, but there was no backing out now. She'd have to press on. "Most brides are so consumed by the idea of marriage they can't fathom the thought of anyone walking away from a potential proposal."

Vera didn't have to contemplate. "I simply do not feel it's the only route for a girl to take, and I can speak from experience. Had Lionel not been taken from me—from all of us," she said, her eyes flicking between Rosemary and Stella—"I'd have married him without a second thought. I believe we'd still be besotted with one another to this day. Freddie, however, is an entirely different man. Had it been he and I who were betrothed at nineteen, well, it wouldn't have gone so well." She shivered at the thought.

"People change. I'm different than I was then, and so is he. We found our way to one another when we were older and had learned a few lessons. I know we'll be truly happy for the rest of our lives. I don't just believe it because I heard it in some fairy tale. I know it to be true, in my heart."

Stella's nose turned red, and her eyes began to water. "Oh,

Vera, that was beautiful."

"It was," Rosemary agreed.

"Oh, for heaven's sake, stop it," Vera demanded. "I am absolutely not turning into a softy, so don't you even suggest it."

Chapter Fourteen

The following day, when Vera exclaimed, "I'm getting married in two days!" the statement wasn't accompanied by grins and giggles. Instead, she looked as though she'd just been delivered a death sentence.

"Yes, dear, I know," Evelyn attempted to soothe, "but Father Davies is ill, and his wife says he simply cannot make it this Sunday." The soothing didn't go off quite as brilliantly as planned because even Evelyn couldn't deny that losing a second clergyman two days before the wedding was cause for considerable concern.

"How can this be happening?" Vera lamented, wailing, her eyes welling with tears. A dramatic reaction, indeed, but authentically Vera nonetheless.

Lorraine made a noise somewhere between a laugh and a grunt. "Who would want to officiate in a church where the last vicar was murdered? Really, why we didn't anticipate this is a mystery."

"Surely there's a clergyman out there somewhere

willing to take your wedding," Evelyn redoubled her efforts to remain cheery, but Rosemary could tell she was reaching the end of her optimism. "Though perhaps on such short notice…" She appeared to have quickly taken a turn and was now following Vera down a rabbit hole.

"Oh, for heaven's sake," Rosemary exclaimed, exasperated. "The answer is right under our noses. Kit Weatherford is qualified, capable, and just down the lane."

Vera beamed at Rosemary as though she'd just invented the cure for Polio right there on the spot rather than merely solved a problem with a painfully obvious solution. "Oh, Rosie, you're right!"

Rosemary shook her head and waved away Vera's admiration. "I'll go see if I can track him down and then Vera and I will make a heartfelt appeal. You all finish your breakfast."

She took a seat at the telephone table in the hall, leaning her head against her hand as she waited to be connected.

Kit's mother, a kindly but harried-sounding lady, thought her son had gone to the church, or perhaps it had been the vicarage—terrible tragedy to have befallen the vicar, of course—in an attempt to comfort Belle.

The way she said it made it sound as though she was unaware the two had parted ways, but she hurried off the telephone before Rosemary had a chance to ask any

142

further questions.

And what questions would she have asked, anyhow? Prying into the romantic relationships of utter strangers was a job for someone like Vera. She shrugged off the urge to satiate her curiosity and instead placed the receiver back in its cradle and poked her head back into the dining room.

"Let's go, bride-to-be. It may just be your lucky day."

Vera sprang from her seat to follow Rosemary. "At last, something productive to do."

"Might I suggest you ladies take an umbrella?" As smoothly as always, Jessop anticipated their needs and stood ready to open the front door. In his hand, he held two umbrellas—one in black, the other the color of ripe plums.

Vera took the black one as, to her way of thinking, black is a color that goes with anything, leaving the other for Rosemary despite the clashing with her pale pink frock.

"Is this new?" Rosemary brandished the umbrella towards Jessop. "I don't remember seeing it before."

"I couldn't say, Miss." If his response seemed a tad reluctant, Rosemary put it down to a reluctance to comment on his mistress's shopping habits.

Vera seemed lighter in her mood as they sped down the drive. This trip was, Rosemary had to admit, far less jarring than the one a few days prior. In preparation for the wedding, Lorraine had arranged for the driveway to undergo a thorough raking to remove the many holes and leave it smoothed to perfection.

When they pulled into the churchyard, there was Fergus, the gardener's son, tending to a small planting that had been beaten nearly to the ground by the driving rain. Beside him lay a pile of trimmings, and one half of the bush—now significantly perkier than the other—proved his efforts were already being rewarded.

He raised a hand politely and then turned back to his work, but when Rosemary stopped the car and stepped out, he approached and asked, "Anything I can do for you ladies?"

"Yes, we're looking for Kit Weatherford," Vera explained. "Have you seen him around? We were under the impression he was visiting the vicarage today."

"He is, yes," Fergus said with a nod. "But he's not in the vicarage. It's just Belle—I mean, Miss Dawson and Mrs. Melville in today." He blushed as his eyes flicked to the cottage. "Kit—or I suppose that would be Father Weatherford now, is in the rectory, most likely, practicing the eulogy."

It hadn't occurred to Rosemary that Kit might be the one to speak at Father Dawson's funeral, which was slated to take place the following day—Saturday, one day before Vera and Frederick were to be wed in the very same church.

She felt a pang of pity for Vera's sake but told herself it happened all the time. People died and were wed every day of the week, after all. Admitting her mother had been correct on that count really irked.

From entirely out of the blue, Fergus blurted, "It was my fault, you know. The vicar's death."

A chill stole over Rosemary's limbs. Had Fergus just confessed to murder?

"How so?" she prodded. Beside her, Vera's body gave off a sense of tension as if she'd become a tightly coiled spring.

"On the night poor Father Dawson died, I'd realized I'd taken the wrong book from the rectory, but when I came to return it, he was busy, and I didn't want to bother him, so I just went into the rectory—without asking, mind you." Fergus bobbed his head and swallowed hard.

No, not a confession—at least not to murder, but it was evident the poor guy had been brooding and needed to unload.

"I'm sure the vicar wouldn't have minded," Vera said, her voice full of sympathy.

"I was right there, wasn't I? When the horrible deed was done. I could have put a stop to it, couldn't I?" Emotion roughened Fergus's voice as the poor lad blamed himself for something he couldn't possibly have foreseen.

Rosemary said as much. "Oh, Fergus. You couldn't have known."

But Fergus would not be comforted. "Father Dawson faced danger while I sat in the rectory and read until the rain slowed down. If only I'd knocked on his door instead of leaving him to his privacy."

Abject misery hung over Fergus like a cloud. Any decent person would have left him alone to let the emotional wound scab over. Instead, Rosemary chose—with some regret—to pick at the painful spot until she'd learned all she could.

"Did you visit the vicarage often?"

Fergus bobbed his head. "My father is a good man, but a simple one. He knows how to grow things, but he never learned to read. Father Dawson loaned me books, and then we'd talk about them after. He called it broadening my horizons."

Vera reached out, laid her hand on Fergus's arm as a gesture of sympathy. "I'm sorry, Fergus. You must miss him terribly."

Again, Fergus bobbed his head. "When the rain slowed, I came out of the church and walked round towards the vicarage. I might have saved him still, but I heard a dog barking." His face reddening in shame, Fergus said, "I don't like dogs much."

"Even so, you mustn't blame yourself for what happened to poor Father Dawson," Rosemary assured, and then let Fergus get back to his pruning.

"How sad," Rosemary said to Vera as she tucked the handle of the umbrella into a more comfortable position in the chook of her arm.

"Quite," Vera replied.

Kit's voice echoed across the sanctuary, and when the sound hit Rosemary's ears, she had to do a double-take to make sure her eyes weren't deceiving her. How such a rich, commanding baritone could emerge from a man who still looked so much like a boy made for a surprising contradiction.

He'd been in the middle of a heartfelt oratory regarding Father Dawson's many redeeming qualities, but he stopped speaking the moment he realized he wasn't alone. "Oh, hello, Miss Blackburn, Mrs. Lillywhite. How may I help you?"

Rosemary had to give him one thing: he didn't forget a name or a face. She couldn't recall having actually been formally introduced and was further impressed.

"We're terribly sorry to intrude," Vera apologized, "but it's rather urgent." Her face pinked as if after the words had left her mouth, she only just realized her predicament probably wouldn't be considered 'urgent' by a man who had just lost his mentor.

Kit didn't seem to mind. He brushed aside the apology with a shake of his head and invited them to take a seat. Once they'd settled, and Rosemary had dispensed with the umbrella by hooking it over the back of the pew, Kit broke the silence.

"Please, tell me how I can be of service."

Vera needed no further prompting. "I was hoping…I mean, I know it's short notice and the timing isn't ideal, but Father Dawson was supposed to take my wedding, and now…well, we don't know what to do. We'd secured Father Davies as he is connected to the parish and agreed to step in, but unfortunately, he's fallen ill."

How Vera could, simultaneously, resemble a beautiful, mythical siren and also a sad, lost puppy dog was an ability Rosemary had always envied. Her charms had been known to work on men, women, the old, and the young, and Reverend Kit Weatherford was no exception.

"Well, I uh," Kit hesitated, "I'm not really uh…"

Vera cut off his hemming and hawing. "You're qualified, are you not?"

"I, uh, wasn't supposed to…thought I'd have more time. But yes," he stuttered. "You are aware I've only just become ordained? Yours would be my first wedding, and I can't guarantee I'd do a brilliant job, particularly given the circumstances."

At this, Vera raised one eyebrow and said, "I don't care

if you recite the ceremony in Hog Latin, whilst hopping on one foot, and waving a banner, so long as when you're through, Freddie and I are officially husband and wife."

Kit considered Vera's statement and, after a few moments of contemplation, smiled a genuine smile—devoid, for the moment, of grief. "I'd be honored to preside over the ceremony," he said, somewhat formally, briefly clasping Vera's hand to seal the deal.

Brilliant, Rosemary thought while Vera and Kit discussed the specifics of the ceremony. She wondered what could have made Belle Dawson turn away from this man who, as far as Rosemary could tell possessed all the qualities one might want in a husband: compassion, loyalty, and patience.

"I can't tell you how grateful I am, I just know you'll make a wonderful job of it." Vera gushed, congenial now that she'd got her own way. "Surely, you've stood before the congregation on many occasions, and you'll deliver the eulogy for Father Dawson. Why would this be so very different?"

Swallowing hard, Kit nodded, then shook his head. "I have, of course, delivered sermons of a Sunday, but Miss. Blackburn, your wedding is the talk of the town. It will be widely attended by strangers."

Vera preened. "It will." And then his meaning hit her. "Oh, I see. You suffer from," she cast about for the appropriate ecclesiastical term, finding none, fell back on the one she knew, "stage fright."

Again, Kit nodded.

"I see," Vera said.

"Father Dawson would tell me to buck up and face my fears no matter what adversity I might face. He'd tell me to listen to my head but follow my heart, no matter the consequences."

"No offense to Father Dawson, but that's," Vera stopped herself from using a word most inappropriate to both the location and the company. "Bad advice."

As it was, the tips of Kit's ears burned red.

"When you're facing a large audience, you need to find a way to make them seem less threatening. Some of my cast members say they simply imagine the audience in their underwear."

Young Father Weatherford nearly choked, Rosemary gasped. "Vera, honestly."

"Oh, sorry," Vera shrugged. "But it is a legitimate method if far too scandalous for this situation. Nevertheless, you get the idea."

Kit himself didn't appear entirely convinced. In fact, his expression a mixture of pain and embarrassment.

"I think we should leave now, Vera. Before you say something else you shouldn't."

When Rosemary glanced backward on the way out of

the chapel, Kit sat staring out into the nave, his brow deeply furrowed. She hoped he could keep it together long enough to officiate the wedding and then felt like an absolute monster for even thinking such an insensitive thought.

She was so wrapped up in self-recrimination she didn't hear Vera's question until the third time she'd repeated it. "Rosie, I asked if you thought we ought to drop in on Belle, see how she's faring. After all, we haven't seen her since the day...well, since her father passed away."

"Yes, of course," Rosemary agreed and followed Vera along the path that led around the back of the church and into the vicarage garden. Fergus had finished his labors or moved along to another area, but the sound of a muted female voice met their ears before the vicarage came in sight.

"Where has that blasted thing gone?" The sight of Cleo Holmes walking across the exact spot where Father Dawson had died made Rosemary shiver. A sixth sense had her pulling Vera to a stop so she could watch. What was the woman doing?

Cleo seemed to be searching for something as she bent to rustle and peer under the shrubbery.

"What's she doing?" Vera hissed in Rosemary's ear, received a shrug for an answer.

After circling the area twice, Cleo approached the

vicarage door and gave it a rap. "Hello, the house," she called out. "Belle, are you in there? Have you seen Dash? Do you mind if I search the premises?"

"Imagine bothering Belle with something so trivial at a time like this."

Mrs. Melville said something of the same when she came to the door, informed Cleo that she'd given Belle a sleeping powder, didn't give a fig whether Dash turned up or not.

"He's a menace, he is," she said. "Digs in the flower beds, steals laundry off the line, and bedeviled the poor vicar with his attention." Then, when it hit Mrs. Melville the vicar was no longer there, her face shuttered. "Search wherever you want. I don't care."

"So much for our good intentions," Vera tugged Rosemary back towards the front of the church. "Can I confess something?"

"Of course," Rosemary answered.

"I feel frivolous for being so happy while Belle is so sad, and I know I should postpone the wedding, but I want to marry your brother more than anything."

"Life goes on, Vera. With all the ups and downs, the happy times, and the sad. It's the way of things. Nobody knows that more than I do. You don't deserve your happiness any less because someone else is going through a bad time."

The sky darkened for a moment as a dark cloud passed by. Probably more rain, Rose thought, and then, she realized she'd left the purple umbrella in the church, and while Vera waited near the car, hurried back for it.

Poor Kit sat where they'd left him, in exactly the same position. Rosemary tiptoed in and retrieved the umbrella quietly so as not to disturb the contemplation of his misery. She had every faith he would pull through the marriage ceremony with flying colors.

Exiting the church, she triumphantly held up the umbrella to show Vera. "I found it."

"Isn't that a lovely umbrella?" Cleo had come around the corner of the church building as Rosemary appeared. "Such a bright shade and so cheerful."

"Thank you," Rosemary said absently.

"Poor Belle. Do you know she hasn't left the house for two days? Cleo pulled her attention from the umbrella and focused on Rosemary's face. "Two days," she emphasized. "I'm worried about her."

With effort, Rosemary schooled her features to keep from showing the incredulity Cleo's statement evoked. The woman before her seemed entirely different from the cranky one she'd met days earlier. Which one was the true Cleo?

"It's to be expected, is it not, after what Belle has gone through."

When Cleo did not get the response she expected, she said, "You haven't seen a little white dog running loose, have you? His name is Dash and he's a German Spitz."

Remembering the bright-eyed pup she'd seen in front of the teashop, Rosemary answered truthfully. "Not today. I'm sorry."

"Well, if you should see him, could you let me know? I live just down from the vicarage."

"Of course," Rosemary said and nodded to Vera, who waved impatiently for her to hurry up. She left Cleo standing alone in front of the church.

"What was all that about? Vera asked.

"Nothing important. Let's get home, shall we." Buoyed by the good news, Vera's spirits stayed high up until a completely snockered Frederick rang to inform Vera he was completely snockered.

"Yes, Freddie, dear. I can hear that for myself," she rolled her eyes, and when he rang off mid-sentence, said to Rosemary, "Remind me again, why did I say yes to your fool of a brother?"

Chapter Fifteen

Breakfast Saturday morning was a tense affair, to say the least—and for a few moments, Rosemary couldn't think why. All the kinks had been ironed out, and everything was on schedule for Vera and Frederick's wedding the following day.

And yet, there Vera sat with a frown on her face. There had been no exclamation this morning, no counting of the hours until she became a wife.

Rosemary hoped Vera wasn't having second thoughts or a case of cold feet, but the jingling of the telephone coincided with, and effectively rendered moot, her conviction to poke the bear. The bear being, that is, a potentially angry bride less than twenty-four hours before her wedding.

In fact, the ringing of the telephone might just have saved Rosemary from mortal peril as it jarred her out of one line of thought and into another. The reason for Vera's plummeting mood became clear.

In a matter of hours, the residents of Pardington would gather to pay their final respects to Father Dawson.

"Miss Rose," Jessop summoned just as she opened her mouth. "There is a call for you," he intoned, giving no further information such as the identity of the caller.

"Hello," Rosemary said into the receiver.

It was Frederick's voice that greeted her on the other end of the line. "Rosie." He sounded pained, and Rosemary felt her heart sink.

"What did you do?" she demanded through clenched teeth. "Besides drinking your weight in gin?"

"I'd really appreciate it, Rose, if for once you could come down off your high horse," her brother said warily as if the mere act of speaking caused him actual physical pain. "I require your assistance, but I'll opt out of the lecture if you don't mind. It seems Simon is a lost cause."

Rosemary wanted to shout but couldn't, lest Vera overhear the conversation, and so she quietly seethed. "What do you mean by lost cause?"

Simon might not be the life of the party, but he was a decent bloke who maybe needed a little spit added to his polish. Calling him a lost cause seemed a step too far, even for Frederick.

Then the play on words got through. "Are you telling me you lost him? Never mind, I already know the answer to that question. Frederick, honestly. It's Pardington.

How lost could he be?"

"It isn't precisely that he's *lost*," Frederick hedged, "Except he is because I don't know where to find him. It's more that he's been distracted, and I'm not entirely certain we'll be *able* to get him back. You see, there was this doll, and she sort of took a shine to our boy Simon. Odd, that, I'd have thought her entirely out of his league."

"Did she," Rosemary said through clenched teeth, "perhaps *take a shine* after you so helpfully informed her that Simon is the heir to mother's family fortune?"

It was scary how well she knew Frederick and even scarier to think he was poised to be married the following day. She hoped Vera's opinion regarding reproduction was shared by her brother and that they'd hold off bringing a miniature Frederick into the world until the full-sized one had grown a lick of common sense.

He was silent for a fraction of a second. "Let's not split hairs, Rosemary. Why don't you just come help me find him? You are the best at solving problems. I need your help," he wheedled. "And you can't tell Vera. I vaguely remember my drunken telephone call from last night, and I suspect she's none too pleased with me as it is."

Rosemary paused for a few moments, considering, and then a few more just to grate on her brother's nerves.

"Fine. I'll come, and I won't say a word to Vera," she replied sweetly before lowering her voice and hissing, "but I'm bringing Mother." With that, Rosemary hung up, silently cursing her brother and his infantile behavior.

Rosemary returned to the table with a forced serene expression plastered on her face, and Vera, bless her heart, was so consumed with her own worries she didn't even bother to ask who had called or why.

Outside, a rumble of thunder in the distance only amplified the feeling of foreboding in Rosemary's stomach. She had a sinking feeling Frederick's shenanigans were going to cost her the better part of a day and the very last of her patience.

"I truly hope Freddie has planned our honeymoon somewhere hot and sunny where I won't have to feel a single raindrop for the whole month," Vera grumbled, staring disgustedly out the window.

Stifling the desire to snort over the idea her brother, who couldn't keep track of an entire human being, might have had the forethought to arrange a suitable honeymoon, Rosemary smiled in Vera's general direction.

"You know, darling Vera, some consider rain on your wedding day as a sign of impending fertility. Could be we'll count the months until you and Frederick celebrate your new life together with a new life entirely." Rosemary kept her tone light and congratulatory, but her eyes twinkled.

"Should that come to pass, darling Rose, I shall remind you of this moment with great frequency, and I shall tell any such new life that Auntie Rose is a witch who curses those she loves with things they are not ready to have."

Vera offered Rosemary a cheeky smile, then tucked back into her eggs with a furrowed brow, but said no more on the subject of rain. It seemed she'd run out of ways to complain about the weather, or perhaps it had finally occurred to her that try as she might, she still couldn't control it.

"I'm afraid I must steal mother away for a short while this morning. We'll be back in time to go with you to the funeral."

Vera grumbled but eventually declared she wished to experiment with hairstyles for the big day. Once she'd gone, Rosemary explained the Simon situation to her mother, and the pair readied themselves to meet Frederick in the village. It was the last place Simon had been seen and the most logical place to begin the search.

With the thrum of the downpour beating on the roof and Jessop occupied elsewhere, Rosemary detoured to the coat cupboard, chose an umbrella for herself, and another for Evelyn.

Amongst the traditional navy and black nestled the pretty purple one she'd used the day before, big enough for two, its handle carved with the head of a bird. Leave it to Lorraine Blackburn to ferret out a designer umbrella.

Even with the enormous umbrella, Rosemary's shoes were soaking by the time she made it into the car, and Evelyn's too.

"Sometimes it thrills me to no end that Frederick is, ultimately, Vera's problem now," Evelyn confessed once they were on the road heading towards Pardington village.

Rosemary held back a snort. "I believe that's entirely fair, Mother, and completely justified."

Evelyn let out a rare chuckle and didn't even say anything uncomplimentary about Rosemary's hair or her outfit on the way to the village.

"I told Freddie we'd meet him at the pub. Return to the scene of the crime, so to speak," Rosemary explained as she stopped the car. She found it highly unlikely Evelyn Woolridge had ever seen the inside of a pub—and was certain if she had, it had been at a reasonable time of day—surely not in the stark light of morning.

Without hesitation, Evelyn followed her daughter inside, though she couldn't hold back the expression of disdain or keep her nose from tilting, ever so slightly, towards the ceiling.

Rosemary called it a win and looked around for Frederick. She spotted him at the far end of the pub, talking with one of the last people she'd ever expected to resort to drinking his troubles away: the new vicar, Kit Weatherford.

Had Evelyn retained enough breath upon seeing the sight, she'd have torn a strip of hide from her son without lifting so much as her little finger. Because she'd been rendered speechless, probably for the first time in her life, it fell to Rosemary to do the deed.

After a long look at the man she supposed she should now refer to as Father Weatherford, Rosemary glared at her brother. "Frederick Woolridge, how could you?"

The disappointment conveyed by her quiet question cut deeper than had she been sharp with him. Frederick clutched his chest as if pained. "I swear upon my honor, this was not my fault."

It had never occurred to him how much his sister and his mother resembled one another until confronted with both of them giving him the same disbelieving look. Wisely, he refrained from commenting on the similarity.

"As if losing Simon wasn't bad enough. The man is a member of the clergy. What were you thinking?" Stepping closer, Rosemary gave in to the urge to pinch her brother. Twice.

"Ow, Rosie!" He slapped her hand away but gently. "Leave off, would you? How was I supposed to know the man had the constitution of a thimble?"

"How much did you give him?" Hands on her hips,

Rosemary demanded loudly.

Blurry-eyed and scruffy, Frederick winced, put a hand to his head. "Have a bit of mercy, sister mine. He's had half a glass, and no more, of the pub's finest gin."

"Half a glass?" Given Kit looked as though he'd been on a week-long siege, Rosemary could be forgiven for doubting her brother's veracity. "Or half a pitcher?"

"Half a glass," young Father Weatherford groaned and forced Rosemary to let Frederick off the hook. "The half touched by the devil himself."

"You see," Frederick said. "Not my fault."

"I let my worries get the better of me and came by for something to eat. I thought food would stop my belly jumping. I ran into Frederick, and he offered me a glass thinking the gin would have a calming effect."

"Rather, not entirely my fault," Frederick amended. "How was I to know he never touched the stuff before?"

"Now, I shall compound my foolishness by presenting the worst eulogy in history. I've let down the congregation and Father Dawson."

"Nonsense!" Surprising everyone, Evelyn spoke briskly. "There's no shame in having a single drink. What you need is some food and something to drink."

Young Weatherford moaned at the word.

"I meant tea," Evelyn huffed.

However, the word tea reminded Rosemary of Mrs.

Shropshire and her magic hangover cure. "Help me get him to the tearoom, Mother if you please."

"I'll do it," Frederick tried to stand, bobbled, and sat back down. "Or not."

Evelyn practically drilled a finger through her son's arm. "Stay here. We will come back for you."

"We've a matter requiring some discretion," Rosemary quickly explained what had happened once she and her mother had settled the new vicar at a corner table, the one farthest from the door and least easily seen through the window. "He's indulged himself a bit too freely with the drink, and I thought you might—"

"Say no more," Mrs. Shropshire said, "I'll mix up a batch of my morning-after specialty, have him fixed right up in no time, and see to it he's at the church on time. "

Leaving Kit in Mrs. Shropshire's capable hands, the Woolridge family moved on to the next item on the list: cousin Simon.

A thorough search of all the shops proved futile, as Simon was nowhere to be found. Frederick checked the park, and a few spots around town where he had, prior to mending his ways, spent a few drunken nights sleeping off a few too many.

Finally, even Evelyn had to admit they were wasting time. "It's wet and cold. Simon isn't out here. He's probably tucked up somewhere, warm and snug, and he'll come back when he's ready. After all, he's a grown man now."

Rosemary and Frederick shared a look of shock but decided, wordlessly, that if their mother was satisfied, that was good enough for them.

When Frederick clamored into the back of her car Rosemary stared at him in astonishment.

"What, you can't give your dear brother a lift back to the house? I'll pay for the petrol, Rosie if it's such an inconvenience."

"What about the funeral?"

"Not going," Frederick replied. "Vera will attend, and it's bad luck to see her before the wedding."

A convenient excuse.

"Must admit," Frederick mused, a hint of slur still coloring his speech, "might be a lark to see a drunk vicar perform a funeral."

"I believe you're angling to burn in hell, Frederick, dear," Evelyn said sharply.

Rosemary sped off towards Woolridge House, making sure to hit each and every bump in the road. Before they'd gone a mile, Frederick paled, then went a bit green and had to curl up into a ball on the rear seat.

After an all-too-brief moment relishing the thought of her brother enduring a painful hangover, Rosemary's attention was drawn to the side of the road. "Oh, bloody hell," she said under her breath as she pulled off onto the muddy verge.

"Simon," Rosemary hollered out the driver's side window. "What on earth are you doing?"

Frederick, hearing Rosemary's exclamation, rose up from where he'd been dozing, his hair a disheveled mess, and opened one eye.

When he saw his cousin walking, barefoot, down the edge of the road, he cracked the other one and nodded approvingly. "Spiffing show, old boy," he said, perking slightly until a positively lethal glance from his mother stilled his tongue.

Next to Simon, held by a makeshift leash, pranced Cleo's dog. Filthy with mud, the little beast quivered with excitement and showed absolutely no remorse for having run wild the entire week.

On the other hand, Simon looked as though he might like to burrow directly into the ground when he noticed the car and realized his aunt Evelyn occupied the passenger seat.

It took all of Rosemary's willpower not to burst out laughing. He stood and stared as if unsure whether to get in or not.

As Simon looked so miserable, Rosemary chose to alight and take control of the dog before it got away again. She grabbed hold of the sodden and muddy item Simon had tied round the dog's neck and tugged gently in the direction of the car.

Dash ran in front of her and leaped, slapped muddy paws against the front of Rosemary's borrowed Mackintosh, and her heart melted. "You poor thing, you're covered in mud. You're rather adorable, aren't you? Let's go."

The little dog obeyed, and in fact, hopped inside the car and settled next to Evelyn on the middle seat. Rosemary ignored her mother's wrinkled nose, climbed in beside Dash, and handed over the leash.

"Simon, where did you get this?" Evelyn asked curiously.

"What?" Simon blinked several times before focusing properly on his aunt. "Oh, I'm…" he paused to dredge the memory up from out of the pool of booze befuddling his brain. "The dog had it when I found him. He was a bugger to catch, but I couldn't leave him out in the rain."

Rosemary glanced to her left, where Evelyn was still studying the strip of fabric. "What is it, Mother?"

"I recognize that color, but I can't imagine how Dash would have come by the belt to Lottie Lewis's raincoat. Nobody else would choose one in that hideous shade of pea green."

It was as though Rosemary had been slapped in the face. "That's the belt that was used to strangle Father

Dawson." The words tumbled out of her mouth before she'd had a chance to think the statement through. Somehow, though, she knew she was right.

"But…" Evelyn stuttered. "How?"

Several scenarios of how Dash might have got hold of the thing ran through Rosemary's mind.

None of them painted a good picture of Lottie.

Chapter Sixteen

At Rosemary's request, Simon got into the backseat and duly avoided Evelyn's gaze.

She granted him some semblance of dignity by keeping her eyes on the road, though whether it was out of courtesy for Simon or a desire not to have the image of his incorrectly buttoned shirt seared into her memory for all time was up for debate.

"I seem to have lost my billfold," he blurted out of nowhere; Rosemary assumed in an attempt to explain why he hadn't hired a cab, but perhaps the loss had something to do with the girl Frederick had mentioned. "And nobody answered the telephone at Woolridge House."

That statement—out of all the others that ought to have caused concern—was what raised Evelyn's hackles. "What do you mean, nobody answered?"

"Well," Simon stuttered, becoming more distressed as the moments passed.

"Mother," Rosemary interjected, "I'd recommend you don't tug at that thread. What's the worst that could happen? They've made their own bed, might as well let them lie in it."

Evelyn considered the suggestion until the car pulled into the drive. "All right, Rosemary. I'll wash my hands of the lot of them."

Being Evelyn, she couldn't, however, simply leave it at that.

"Frederick Woolridge, you had better make sure my house is put back exactly the way I left it, do you hear?" Rosemary heard her say to her brother as he slunk out of the car. "And you can tell your father he can't avoid me forever. I'll see him tomorrow at the wedding. Remind him of that."

Frederick nodded, and when he turned to walk away, she could see a look of pure terror on his face. Rosemary guessed it was a good thing her brother would be taking off on his honeymoon before Evelyn returned to Woolridge House.

She suspected this still wasn't enough to demote him from his place as their mother's favorite child and shook her head ruefully at the thought.

After Frederick and Simon disappeared into the house, Evelyn looked towards Rosemary and burst out laughing.

"Are you quite mad?" Rosemary asked, which only

seemed to spur her mother on. The laughter, however inappropriate, proved infectious because it wasn't long before Rosemary began to giggle.

Dash woke, cocked his head to one side, and looked between them both curiously. After a moment, he let out a bark as if trying to join in, and the sound instantly sobered both Evelyn and Rosemary.

"Oh, dear," Evelyn breathed. "I don't know what got into me, but I feel better now, don't you?"

Rosemary, for once, didn't hate admitting Evelyn was right. "Oddly, I do. Though, I suggest neither of us tell anyone what we just did. It might come off as...insensitive."

"My, yes," Evelyn agreed. It wasn't often she and her mother found themselves in cahoots, and Rosemary was surprised to discover it felt nice.

Evelyn gestured to the dog and the raincoat belt. "Now, what shall we do about this?"

"Unfortunately, we need to go see the inspector," Rosemary replied with a sigh. "We've barely time. There's only one thing to be done. Wait here and make sure Dash doesn't make another break for it."

She left Evelyn in the car and tiptoed inside, resisting the urge to peek into the rooms and assess the damage Frederick and the rest of the men had inflicted. If she didn't see anything, Rosemary reasoned, she wouldn't have to say anything.

Instead, she made a beeline for the telephone stand and dialed the Blackburn estate, giving Jessop swift instructions and then disconnecting the line.

"Rose," she heard a familiar stage whisper from the doorway to the parlor. "What are you doing here?" It was Max, and he looked quite handsome with his hair mussed as it was.

Rosemary did her best to explain, promising to give him all the details as soon as she could.

"Shall I break out of here and come to the funeral with you?" Max asked. "Surely Freddie won't notice if I leave."

"He will, and it's not worth it. You didn't know Father Dawson—I hardly knew him, either, but I can't get out of it. There's no reason for you to suffer, too." She kissed him soundly and then sneaked back out the door.

Assuring her mother she'd seen to things, Rosemary pulled out of the drive and turned towards the village. She wished she could simply drop the dog and the belt with the police department secretary and be on her way, but of course, that wouldn't do at all, and Evelyn would never have allowed it.

As it turned out, her mother's presence was a blessing—as it had been, repeatedly, all morning. Inspector Trousseau was on his best behavior and made not one cheeky remark during the brief conversation.

Together, they explained how cousin Simon had come to find Dash, recognized him as Cleo Holmes' missing German Spitz, and lured him close with a piece of jerky he'd happened, on a stroke of providence, to have tucked away in his pocket.

The inspector had appeared somewhat bemused by the first portion of the tale, but it was the second part that really caught his attention.

He sat up in his desk chair and leaned forward when Rosemary presented him with the raincoat belt, and Evelyn piped up to testify she'd seen the same one on Lottie Lewis at church a week before the vicar's death.

"That's enough evidence for me to make an arrest on suspicion," Trousseau had pronounced, standing up and taking his coat from the back of his chair.

Rosemary, with a glance at the clock, urged, "Please, if Lottie is already at the church, couldn't you wait until after the service to make your arrest? It would be in poor taste to do so before." If she'd batted her eyelashes just a tiny bit, it was for a good cause, even if it did make her want to gag.

A look in his eyes that would have boiled Max's blood—Rosemary tended to deny her effect on men could and often did rival that of Vera's—Inspector Trousseau agreed to wait and walked out behind her and Evelyn as they hurried to the exit.

"Wait," turning back to address the constable on duty, Rosemary said, "What about the dog?" She couldn't bear the thought of leaving the adorable little pooch behind, especially while he stared balefully at her with those inquisitive little eyes.

"Don't worry," the constable replied. "I'll make sure he gets back home safe and sound. He is a fetching little thing, isn't he?" It was enough for Rosemary, and there wasn't time to argue.

***

Evelyn proved herself less uptight than ever when she didn't even protest over Rosemary's plan to change their clothes for the funeral in the loo at Mrs. Shropshire's tearoom. Jessop had delivered on Rosemary's instructions in their entirety, and Vera and Lorraine had arrived carrying everything she'd requested in two large garment bags.

When they were dressed and ready, every hair in place, with just enough time to make it to the church, Rosemary finally breathed a sigh of relief. Finding Simon was one problem solved; now, if the problem of Father Dawson's drunken eulogist had also resolved itself, perhaps the day wouldn't be a complete disaster.

Aside, of course, from the imminent arrest that Rosemary herself had facilitated. At least this time, her involvement had been circumstantial and, furthermore, accidental. She'd happily blame it all on Simon if Vera gave her any trouble.

To Rosemary's surprise, she received none, and in fact, Vera appeared contrite regarding her behavior earlier that morning.

"It's a bride's prerogative to be ornery and difficult," Rosemary had assured her friend. "Nonetheless, I'm glad to see you've snapped out of your persnickety mood," she added with a wink.

Since this was no Sunday service, the seating arrangements were thrown into upheaval. Parishioners who usually occupied the front of the nave had no claim, as even though Father Dawson hadn't much family to speak of, they still took up the first rows of pews.

Mrs. Melville sat in a seat behind Belle and kept her hand gripped tightly on the girl's shoulder in such a way it was unclear whether she was providing comfort or seeking it herself.

Those with whom the vicar had little to no relationship—yet still felt obliged to attend the service—sat in the back, and would leave as soon as it ended.

It was the territory in the middle that had turned into a battle zone. Even during an event as solemn as a funeral, the cogs of Pardington's social machine continued to grind.

Those who fancied themselves on intimate terms with the vicar—which as such, in their minds, put them that much closer to God—fought to sit as near the front as possible.

One particular group, including Cleo Holmes and a handful of the ladies from the previous week's post-church service gathering, pressed into one row like a line of sausages, so reluctant were any of them to take a seat in the next pew back.

The tussle remained dignified and didn't, Rosemary noticed, devolve to fisticuffs, but she wouldn't have been at all surprised if it had.

Rosemary counted herself lucky her party held no illusions and simply took the closest spot available upon their arrival. *God looks down*, her mother had been known to say, *and we all look the same from above*. Funny how that adage didn't seem to apply anywhere besides church.

"Look, there she is now," Evelyn whispered to Rosemary and shivered. The *she* was Lottie, barely recognizable in a black dress and veil. She loitered at the back and attempted to fade into the woodwork.

The sight of her filled Rosemary with unease.

"Perhaps you oughtn't to have talked Inspector Trousseau into waiting until after the service," Evelyn helpfully pointed out. "It's morbid for the murderer to attend the funeral."

Rosemary hadn't really thought of it that way as concern for Belle's feelings had driven the request for the inspector's patience. The girl ought to have the chance to grieve her father without distraction. Now, she wondered if she had made the wrong choice. Unfortunately, it was too late, as Kit took his place behind the pulpit, and the twittering subsided into silence.

Kit's appearance proved—redundantly, as both Rosemary and Vera could have attested to the fact—that Mrs. Shropshire was a magician when it came to hangover cures.

Whatever she'd forced down his throat had done the trick. If there were lines around his eyes, they could be chalked up to grief and the strain of delivering the eulogy, but she doubted anyone would have cause to question in the first place.

He delivered a beautiful sermon, citing quotes he'd collected directly from Father Dawson, and it was almost as if the vicar himself were speaking through his protege.

"We are never truly gone, for we all leave our mark. Be it with our words, our actions, our love, or our service, every soul sears the earth with its own unique imprint— something to pass on to the next generation. That was what Father Dawson believed, and I think we can all

agree what he left for us won't soon be forgotten," Kit finished solemnly. "Now, let us pray."

It was a wonder Belle made it through the service without falling to pieces. She stood stiffly, her face giving nothing away even as she watched a solemn Fergus and the other pallbearers carry her father's casket down the aisle and out the church doors towards the graveyard and his final resting place.

Rain, fined down to a light mist, fell soft upon the mourners as nature couldn't bear to add more weight to the moment. The procession followed solemnly, Belle following closely behind Father Dawson.

She was flanked by Delilah and Hyacinth, the pair of them holding onto her tightly enough that when her knees went weak, they could keep her upright.

Would Lottie's arrest bring Belle closure or rip the still-raw wound open again? Rosemary sincerely hoped for the former, taking comfort in the fact she'd have her friends to help her through the tough times ahead.

Vera wrapped one arm around Rosemary's waist, put her other hand on the umbrella handle, and matched pace with her friend to remain in the small circle of dry shelter.

When Inspector Trousseau hailed Lottie on her way to the graveside, Rosemary's breath caught in her throat. Surely he didn't mean—

"Lottie Lewis, I'm hereby placing you under arrest for

the suspected murder of Reverend Horatio Dawson."

Quite a few guests had taken the opportunity to bow out of the second part of the service, and therefore the group who got to watch Lottie be placed in handcuffs and informed of her rights was somewhat smaller than it might have been.

Even so, Rosemary felt the sudden urge to verbally eviscerate Inspector Trousseau. He'd stuck to the letter of his promise and had indeed waited until after the funeral. However, in her eyes, his choice of timing showed his true colors, and they were all ugly shades of baby nappy green.

Belle stood, now of her own volition, her hands clenched at her sides, watching as Lottie was loaded into the back of Trousseau's police car. She wore an enigmatic expression somewhere between satisfaction, disgust, and pain.

At the end of the committal service, Hyacinth materialized in front of Rosemary and Vera. "Aunt Lorraine has agreed to let us bring Belle back for the night, only if you have no objection. She can't bear to stay another night in the vicarage. I know it's your wedding tomorrow, but I do hope you'll say yes."

"Never let it be said Vera Blackburn turned away anyone in a time of need. By all means, bring Belle along for the night."

"Thank you," Hyacinth frowned at Vera as if seeing her for the very first time. "I promise Belle won't be any bother. I expect she'll take a sleeping powder straight after dinner, so you won't even know she's there."

"I've said yes, have I not? Belle is welcome to stay and to whatever peace of mind she might derive from being among friends."

"What was that all about?" Rosemary wanted to know.

Vera shrugged. "I'm sure she expected me to play the heartless child and say no."

Hyacinth's prediction proved correct as Belle, pale and wan from an emotionally exhausting day, excused herself directly following dinner.

"We'll come with," Delilah insisted, and all three went upstairs.

Several hours later, Rosemary and Vera finally followed suit, but instead of sleeping powders and sweet dreams, they settled in front of the fireplace to chat.

"After tomorrow, everything will be different," Vera stared into her crystal tumbler, then circled it to swirl the half-inch of gin around the bottom.

"It will," Rosemary agreed. "Are you having second thoughts?" She rested tired feet on a tufted stool and waited for the answer.

"Not at all. Did you? When it was your turn with Andrew?"

Wryly, Rosemary said. "It crossed my mind for a split second that perhaps I was making a mistake. Then I thought of his face and realized I'd be crazy to walk away."

"You would have been," Vera agreed. "Would you go back and do it again, if you knew how it would end?"

"A hundred times over. It seems an age since then. So much has changed." Nostalgia brought the sting of tears. "Frederick is a good man. He's often a fool, but I believe he will do his best by you."

"As I plan to do the same, that certainly warms my heart." Vera tipped up her glass and swallowed the clear spirits. "We shall become sisters tomorrow, and that is no bad thing in itself."

"Well," said Rosemary, "It's good to know that not everything will change." So saying, she rose, kissed Vera on the top of the head, and made her way to bed, leaving the bride-to-be a moment of solitude.

CHAPTER SEVENTEEN

Rosemary wasn't sure how it happened, but everything related to Vera's wedding fell into place the morning of the event. The solarium had been set nearly to perfection the previous evening. Round tables encircled a central area in the middle of the room, which would serve as a dance floor later in the evening when the sun had gone down, and tens of dozens of tiny pinprick lights twinkled overhead.

All of the flower arrangements had arrived before most of the household had awakened, and now nary a surface inside the Blackburn estate went unadorned with blooms. Vera had shrugged off her doldrums and floated around the house all morning as if on a cloud.

Rosemary left her in the bedroom, which looked as though the makeup counter at Selfridge's had exploded all over it, having her hair styled and her manicure freshened.

"I've some matron of honor duties to attend to; I trust

you're in good hands," she'd said, to which Vera had waved one finger, the only thing she could move while being poked and prodded from every angle.

When she'd returned, an hour later, having supervised the ironing of the gowns and laid out all of Vera's accessories, she gathered the bride and insisted that before she dress, she eat a decent meal. If the two flutes of champagne Vera had consumed during the primping process had anything to do with the suggestion, Rosemary would never admit it.

Vera's hair did indeed look positively lovely, set in perfect finger curls like lace along one temple. The other would be hidden beneath a stylish satin and lace headpiece, hand-beaded in excruciating detail. Rosemary had no doubt the photos would be gorgeous.

When she and Vera entered the dining room, it was to discover that the table which had, all morning, been home to a roundabout of Blackburn family members and a seemingly bottomless breakfast feast, sat empty.

Instead, huddled near one of the windows facing the side garden stood Evelyn, Lorraine, Kitty, and even Jessop.

"What on earth are you all doing?" Rosemary asked, startling her mother nearly out of her skin.

"For heaven's sake, child," Evelyn said, catching her breath.

"I'm afraid we have a wedding crasher," Lorraine explained.

Rosemary peered out the window, her eyes widening when she recognized the figure as Alistair Cox. She noted he didn't look nearly as filled with bravado huddled behind the shrubbery.

"He must be here looking for Belle Dawson," Rosemary said, shrugging. Her stomach had begun to rumble, and the scents of sausage and buttered toast called to her from across the room. Vera had already dug in, raising a slice of bacon carefully to her lips so as not to smudge her makeup.

Kitty snorted, the sound full of contempt, and spat, "Some lady detective you are. You haven't got a clue, do you? He's not here for Belle. He's here," she paused for dramatic effect, "for Hyacinth."

"What about Hyacinth?" Another voice echoed Rosemary's earlier question, its owner having entered the room just in time to hear the tail end of the conversation.

Hyacinth stared at Kitty as she approached the window while Belle and Delilah, who had been on her heels, hung back and exchanged a quizzical look.

Rosemary stepped aside and allowed Hyacinth to shove in. When she caught sight of Alistair, she let out a squeak and then turned and ran out of the dining room. Everyone, save for Jessop, followed her out the front door and around the flagstone path to the side garden.

"Alistair," Hyacinth cried, startling him. He whipped around, momentarily appearing relieved to see her and then equally suspicious of the throng of people trailing behind. "What are you doing here?" she asked, her voice rising to a squeak.

He focused his eyes on her now and took her hands in his. "That inspector has it in for me, Hy. He wants to pin the vicar's murder on me. I have to get out of town."

"No," Hyacinth protested, "he's not"—

"It's bad, Hy. Really bad," Alistair interrupted, beginning to sound desperate. "But you could help me. You know I had nothing to do with the vicar's death, and you have the means to help me get away from here. After I'm gone, you can explain. They'll believe you. Some seed money is all I'd need. Surely you can spot me?"

It was like a train that had veered off its track or one of Vera's more questionable theater productions. No—it was as though he'd taken an introductory acting course and compiled all the lessons he'd learned into one monologue.

The lot of them stood, equally mesmerized by the man's audacity and full of trepidation, wondering what Hyacinth's reaction to his request might be.

Lorraine stepped forward as if to intervene, but Delilah stopped her with a hand. "Aunt Lorraine," she said quietly, "she needs to work this out for herself."

"Is that why you're with me? You think because my name is Blackburn, that automatically means I'm rich?" The squeak had disappeared, and in its place came the voice of a confident young lady who had been pushed to her breaking point. "You should have done your research. I'm not ashamed to say I've no money to speak of."

Alistair looked as though he'd been slapped across the face. He recovered quickly and pulled himself up to his full height, "What now? You'll let me be hanged for a crime I didn't commit? You were there that night, too. I'll take you down with me!"

"Take her down for what, precisely?" Inspector Trousseau's voice pierced the silence left between Alistair's dramatic exclamation and what would have been an explosion of laughter had the incredulous group not been struck dumb by the officer's unexpected arrival.

All heads turned in his direction, identical wide-eyed expressions of shock splayed across each face.

"Your butler telephoned the station twenty minutes ago," Trousseau explained his presence even though nobody had verbalized the question, then turned to Hyacinth and repeated, "Take you down for what?"

"Nothing," Hyacinth snapped, rendering even the inspector surprised, and pierced Alistair with a glare. "You've played your cards too soon. Did you spend the last day sleeping off another bender? If you hadn't, you might have noticed the police already arrested Father Dawson's murderer. You are no longer a suspect."

"Not so fast," Inspector Trousseau said. He took another step closer, and when it looked like Alistair might make a run for it, he pointed to where his young constable stood holding a billy club and leering.

"I've still a few questions I'd like to ask you regarding some outstanding warrants. Ring any bells? Brown, escort Mr. Cox to the station. Put him in cuffs if he gives you any trouble. This guy will con you out of your britches if you give him half a chance."

As Alistair passed by Hyacinth, she tossed her hair and spat, "We're through, in case you still held any illusions." Apparently, he didn't because he kept his mouth firmly closed and his eyes on the ground in front of him.

As soon as Alistair and the constable were out of earshot, the inspector set his gaze upon Hyacinth. "You have some explaining to do, Miss Blackburn," he said through clenched teeth. "Am I to understand *you* left the grounds the night of the vicar's murder? Did you not insist that neither you nor Miss Dawson left your room until morning?"

"No, sir, Inspector Trousseau," Hyacinth insisted eagerly. "You asked me if Belle left. I said she did not. I told the truth. Besides, we didn't see anything, but I was afraid you wouldn't believe Alistair." Hyacinth laughed bitterly. "I'm a fool, but I'm guilty of nothing but choosing the wrong man."

The inspector eyed her and then did something Rosemary never would have expected. "Under the circumstances, I won't press the matter, at least not just yet."

That Trousseau might have felt a smidgen of remorse for the timing of Lottie Lewis's arrest crossed Rosemary's mind.

"However," he continued, "I will need to take your statement—your real statement—and I must warn you, Miss Blackburn, that withholding information is tantamount to lying. You'd do well to remember that lesson."

"That's quite generous of you, Inspector," Lorraine practically purred, linking her arm through his and directing him back towards his automobile. "Why don't you go tend to that," she waved a hand in Alistair Cox's general direction, "and come back for the wedding at one o'clock? It will be the party of the year, I can promise that."

It was a rare soul who possessed the strength to turn down a proposition from Lorraine Blackburn, and Inspector Trousseau wouldn't be counted amongst them.

When she'd shooed him off, she turned and stalked

back, making a beeline for Kitty. All the syrupy sweetness that she'd bestowed upon the inspector had evaporated, and now she was like a cougar stalking its prey.

"I'm ashamed of you, Kitty, and you ought to feel the same about yourself. You have acted positively rotten all week. You were impolite to Rosemary just moments ago, and you've been particularly derisive towards Vera on multiple occasions. You didn't even hesitate to throw your cousin to the wolves the moment you were given an opportunity. What has Hyacinth ever done to you? What have any of us ever done to you, for that matter?"

Kitty's eyes narrowed, and her fists clenched at her sides. "What did you ever do to help any of us? You honestly respond to my question, and then you'll have figured out the answer to yours."

Lorraine looked as though she'd been slapped. "Surely, Kitty, you don't believe"—

"Mother," Vera interrupted. "It's not really the time, is it?" She shook her head, a plea in her eye.

"You don't know what it's been like," Kitty spat at Vera, the floodgates having opened, "to live in the shadow of the great Vera Blackburn. Vera who gets everything she ever wants and still always wants more! You have everything," she cried, "even staff who will lie to the police for you."

Rosemary's head was spinning, and not just from the plethora of information that had been revealed throughout the previous half-hour. She thought she might also have a case of whiplash from trying to keep up with the accusations and insults flying back and forth across the garden.

Vera's serene mood from just a short time ago felt very far away, and Rosemary was at a complete loss for a way to stop the madness.

Lorraine pinned Kitty with a glare. "I've no reason to sling insults, nor as it's my daughter's wedding day much desire. Explain your statement, now."

"Jessop!" Kitty exclaimed, pointing at the butler. "He knows Hyacinth sneaked out the night Father Dawson was killed. Just ask him!"

Lorraine turned to Jessop and raised a brow.

"You're not entirely correct, Miss Kitty, but you're not entirely wrong. I suspected someone left the house after the Dawson girl arrived, but I'd no idea it was Miss Hyacinth. It mattered little which of you it was. I serve the Blackburns—*all* the Blackburns, according to the pledge I made to Mr. Blackburn twenty-two years ago."

"But how did you know?" his mistress demanded an explanation.

Jessop sighed as if reluctant to reveal all his secrets in quick succession. "She left her umbrella in the foyer. I found it and put it away. I thought perhaps it had been from earlier in the evening and therefore felt no need to discuss the matter with the inspector."

It was complete hogwash. Nobody who'd spent any amount of time at the Blackburn house with Jessop believed his eagle eye would have missed an umbrella dripping water all over the foyer floor.

Hyacinth sighed. "I knew I shouldn't have picked up that umbrella. Apologies, Jessop, for putting you in that position."

"You can't be serious!" Kitty exclaimed, but she didn't get a chance to say much else because the bride had finally had enough.

Vera stepped up in front of Kitty and said calmly. "You're mistaken regarding the facts, Katherine. I'd suggest you learn the truth before slinging insults. It's Mother and me who have been treated as lepers, not the other way around. She offered to house all the cousins every summer; it was your parents who refused to allow any more than an occasional weekend."

That bit of information was a revelation to more than Kitty. Rosemary had no idea there'd been any angst behind those weekends she remembered so fondly. And apparently, Lorraine had thought she'd kept it all from Vera.

"How did you know?" she asked her daughter, ignoring

Kitty now.

Vera rolled her eyes skyward. "Please, Mother," she said affectionately, "I'm your daughter through-and-through. Do you really need to ask?"

Lorraine smiled. "I suppose not. Now, Kitty, attend the wedding or not. Be part of the family or not. Do whatever you'd like, but I don't recommend you utter another word unless it's part of a sincere apology."

Kitty considered, her eyes welling with tears, but she didn't say a word and instead stalked off towards the rear garden.

Rosemary pulled Vera close, taking pains not to muss her hair, and murmured, "It's going to be all right. Let's put all that behind us and focus on what's really important. You're getting married in two hours!"

Vera took a deep breath, smiled, and nodded. "You're right, Rosie. I'm not going to let Alistair Cox, or Inspector Trousseau, and especially not Kitty, get me down today. I've invested blood, sweat, and tears into this wedding, and I'm damned well going to enjoy it!"

"Right so!" Rosemary agreed and allowed herself to be pulled back along the footpath to the front of the house.

Stella emerged from the dining room just as she and Vera entered the foyer. It was obvious she'd been curled up somewhere, asleep, her hair on one side matted to her face to prove it in case the stifled yawn hadn't been enough.

"What?" she asked, wide-eyed. "What did I miss?"

***

Rosemary deposited Vera in her bedroom, allowing her a few quiet moments and a chance to freshen up one more time before being trussed into her gown.

She knew there were a thousand details she ought to check on, but instead, she found herself in the library with a glass of brandy in her hand. A few long sips calmed her nerves and made her feel as though she might actually get through the day without facing any more disasters.

As she entered the hallway, an overwhelming sensation of deja vu gripped Rosemary. Hushed voices wafted from the guest room where Hyacinth bunked.

"*I'm* the one who should be sorry, Hy," came Belle's voice, more contrite than Rosemary had ever heard it. Perhaps the shock she'd experienced would ultimately have a positive effect on the girl's disposition.

"He's a scoundrel," she said without mincing words, "but I can see you cared for him. I shouldn't have insinuated there was something between us when there wasn't. Although," Rosemary could imagine Belle's eyes flashing now, "if you'd confided in any of us, I would have known better."

"Why did you lie in the first place?" Hyacinth asked.

Belle didn't answer for a moment. "I was embarrassed. I didn't break things off with Kit. It was he who decided not to marry me. No girl wants to admit to having been thrown over, do they? He didn't even have the guts to tell me to my face. He made Papa do it for him, and because of that, the last words I said to my father were in anger. It wasn't his fault, and I took it out on him like I always did. "

Belle's voice became thick with emotion. "It's my fault. I snapped at Lottie, and then Father defended me to her. Fergus heard enough to know that much, and for some reason, felt the need to unburden himself. I wish he'd never said anything at all, but if he hadn't, Lottie might have walked free."

"Oh, Belle," Hyacinth replied sadly, and Delilah echoed the statement.

"How I wish Father had simply married Mrs. Melville ages ago," she replied, a bitter edge to her voice. "He'd never have been dating Lottie in the first place, and he'd still be alive."

"Why Mrs. Melville?" Delilah asked, surprised.

"Oh, she's been pining after him forever. Since before Mother died even," Belle explained. "You must have noticed. She's never come right out and said it, but I've always been able to tell."

Rosemary crept on, feeling guilty for listening in on yet another conversation in this very same hallway. The feeling didn't last long because it was replaced with one of rueful amusement. What was it about Father Dawson that had got all the Pardington octogenarians in a tizzy?

Had he been a catch? The thought, combined with the brandy, gave Rosemary the last ounce of fortitude she needed to make it through the rest of the day.

Chapter Eighteen

Immediately following the ruckus with Kitty, Lorraine and Evelyn got dressed and drove down to the church to supervise the decorating process. Rosemary promised to gather the wedding party and ensure everyone made it there with plenty of time to spare.

She and the girls changed clothes quickly, each donning a protective cardigan over their dresses at Vera's request. Her fear over the weather had yet to dissolve as the sky continued as it had, all morning, to fluctuate between blue and grey.

The promise might have been easier to keep had not the church car park been far too small for such an event. As a result, the lane leading from it to the Blackburn estate was lined with vehicles, and the trip took twice as long as usual.

Frederick and his ushers had already arrived and were filing towards the entrance when Rosemary pulled up. Vera squeaked and held her arms over her face. "He can't see me yet! It's terrible luck!"

Rosemary felt certain that at this point, her brother catching sight of Vera before she reached the end of the aisle was just another drop in the bucket, but she pulled swiftly into the reserved space between two other cars and blocked Vera from Frederick's view.

"Lilah, Hy, help Vera out of the car," Rosemary instructed. "Mind you don't let her dress drag while I go clear us a path to the rectory."

She did so and then returned to the car park to collect the bride, hefting an accessory case—larger than Rosemary thought could possibly be necessary at this juncture—out of the boot.

Vera grinned as she and the bridesmaids bustled past the set of closed double doors leading to the nave.

"It's a packed house," she said giddily. There wasn't much Vera loved more than having every eye in the room trained on her.

Evelyn peeked her head out of the rectory door and motioned for the girls to hurry. "We've not much time before the guests become restless." She fetched the case from Rosemary, plopped it down on the table, and lifted the lid.

"Something new, check," Vera said, pointing to the elaborate headpiece that had taken so long to design it could nearly have counted as her something old. "This necklace has been in the family for generations, so that's covered, and technically this is a borrowed dress."

Technically, it had been gifted to Vera as a thank you for she and Rosemary having reunited a pair of estranged lovers. The necklace, however, belonged to Lorraine, so Rosemary figured it all came out in the wash.

Evelyn had gone behind Lorraine's back on the sixpence, used an adhesive to attach it to the underside of Vera's shoe so it wouldn't cause a blister, which left only the something blue.

"Where is that handkerchief?" Vera asked, her voice strained and her movements becoming agitated. She rustled about in the case, yanking out several of the pairs of extra stockings and tossing them aside.

The rectory door burst open then, and in raced little Lionel. "Auntie Rose!" he shouted, nearly toppling Rosemary to the floor in his excitement.

"Hey there, little man," she said, bending down to give him a hug and a kiss on each of his soft, pudgy cheeks.

Cleo Holmes entered not far behind Lionel and Stella another moment later. "Thank you, Mrs. Holmes," Stella said breathlessly, "for trying to help. He got away from me," she huffed.

"Oh, it's no trouble," Cleo replied. "I know what it's like to have a rambunctious little one. Talking of, I'd like to tell you ladies how much I appreciate you having found my little Dashy-do," she gushed. "I would have been lost without him. It was a lovely surprise to come home from the funeral yesterday and discover he'd been returned safely."

The woman was as mercurial as the weather, Rosemary thought to herself while absently removing Lionel's hand from the pocket of her cardigan. It was her own fault; she usually kept a few butterscotch sweets in there, and he loved to hunt for them.

Whatever she might have said in reply to Cleo's gratitude was canceled when Vera let out an angry expletive. "It's not here. How can it not be here? That handkerchief was my something blue!" she wailed.

"Oh, dear," Cleo replied, her eyes growing wide with concern. Had the woman been on any more intimate terms with Vera, she'd have known that the bride's middle name ought to have been *melodramatic*.

Evelyn attempted to calm Vera's nerves and save the day, "Surely someone's carrying something blue. Ladies, check your handbags, quickly."

Everyone did, even Cleo, but by some stroke of providence, there wasn't a suitable blue item between them.

"I've a blue handkerchief—hand embroidered, quite beautiful—at my house just across the way. Would you like me to fetch it?" Cleo asked.

Vera considered for a split second and said gratefully, "That would be lovely if it's not too much trouble. You'd be a real lifesaver."

"It's no trouble, dear, though come to think, it's tucked into one of the boxes at the top of my wardrobe. Don't you fret. I'll be back in a jiff."

"Perhaps you'd better just drive back up to the house, Rose," Vera suggested. "There's no need to put Mrs. Holmes out."

Rosemary shook her head. "I'll never make it there and back. Why don't I simply accompany Mrs. Holmes and aid in the search? Unless she objects, of course."

She didn't, and Rosemary followed her path, somewhat impatiently, while Dash barked up a storm. As soon as the door opened, out he rushed, ignoring Cleo entirely to dance around Rosemary's feet.

"Hey there, pup," she said, bending down to give him a scratch behind the ears. He leaned into her hand, and her heart melted a little. Cleo cleared her throat and gestured for Rosemary to step inside.

With one last look at the church—the view from Cleo's front stoop could have been painted on a postcard—Rosemary let the door close behind her.

Inside, the place smelled mildly of dog, the odor somewhat covered by a whiff of turpentine and a cloud of the flowery perfume preferred by church ladies everywhere.

On one wall hung a series of framed oil paintings. "Is this your work?" Rosemary asked, momentarily distracted from her task. "I'd no idea you were an artist. I fancy myself one as well," she explained. "These are simply marvelous."

The arrangement consisted of a sort of mosaic, seven individual works clustered around one central painting. It was apparent Cleo had been inspired by the view of the churchyard from her window. Each of the surrounding images captured a piece of the larger work in more intricate detail.

One small canvas depicted Cleo herself standing near a headstone in the church graveyard. Another, the arbor where poor Father Dawson met his maker. A third, the vicar in his younger days, leaning down as he listened to his daughter. With delicate strokes, Cleo had captured the essence of a cheerful man and an attentive father.

"Oh, it's just a hobby of mine," Cleo brushed off the compliment despite flushing crimson and sounding rather pleased. "I'll go pull out the boxes, and then we can search," she said, disappearing down the hallway towards the rear of the cottage.

After she'd left, Rosemary looked around the rest of the sitting room curiously. On a shelf above the mantle, she spied a faded photograph of a much younger and carefree-looking Mrs. Holmes aside a comely fellow with a mischievous expression. She assumed this was Mr. Holmes and guessed he'd been gone for quite some time.

Rosemary peered down the hallway where Cleo had disappeared and asked, "Any luck?" before glancing back to the mantle where another picture caught her eye.

This one was a charcoal drawing rendered in exquisite detail. It was Father Dawson's face with perhaps a decade's fewer wrinkles. The work was top-notch, and Rosemary couldn't help but admire it.

If it was a tad odd that Cleo had a sketch of the vicar on her mantle, Rosemary didn't think much of it. It was a lovely piece of art, and if it had been her own design, she'd also have desired to display it proudly.

"Mrs. Holmes," Rosemary called, tearing herself away to refocus on the task in front of her. Vera wouldn't dream of walking down the aisle without her something blue, and all she wanted to do now was find the hanky and get back to the church.

Receiving no answer, she ventured down the hallway and poked her head into the slightly ajar door at the end. "Mrs. Holmes," she said again, wondering where on earth her hostess could have disappeared to.

"Oh, dear." Cleo came out of another door— presumably the loo—and started at the sight of Rosemary. "You musn't sneak up on an old lady like that. My heart nearly stopped." Her tone had reverted to the diamond-hard one she'd used at the post-church social the previous Sunday.

"Apologies, Mrs. Holmes," Rosemary stuttered, a sudden chill trailing up her spine. "Did you find the handkerchief?"

"It's in one of these two hat boxes," Cleo replied brusquely. "Why don't you help me look?"

With no choice but to comply—Rosemary now vehemently wished she'd simply driven back to the Blackburn estate to fetch Vera's handkerchief—she began to gingerly sort through a collection of ancient trinkets that looked and smelled as if it hadn't been touched in years.

"Is this it?" Rosemary asked hesitantly, having turned up a molding scrap of blue fabric.

Cleo nodded. "That's it," she confirmed, taking the box from Rosemary. She carried it to the wardrobe and opened the door to reveal a mirror on the other side.

Tucked into the corner of the mirror's frame was a small photograph that appeared as though it had been cut from the newspaper. Realizing it was yet another depiction of Father Dawson's face, Rosemary's stomach dropped to the floor.

And then she saw something that made it flip over onto itself several more times in quick succession: inside the wardrobe leaned an umbrella case in beautifully dyed, plum-colored leather.

Rosemary didn't know what to do. What did it mean? Possibly nothing, she told herself. Could it be a coincidence that the umbrella Hyacinth had left in the Blackburn foyer the night of the vicar's death matched a case that belonged to the vicar's next-door neighbor?

Yes, she told herself, it was possible. Yet, another voice in her head piped in to remind her of the drawing of Father Dawson displayed above the fireplace. Strange, that. Too strange to be considered a coincidence if she were honest.

Nonetheless, there was no time to consider the matter further. The best Rosemary could do was get back to the church and address her suspicions against Cleo after Vera and Frederick had sailed off on their honeymoon.

She took a deep breath and lavished the woman with a smile. If it wavered slightly, Rosemary hoped it could be blamed on the stresses of the day. "Vera will be so grateful. Why don't we get back to the church now? She's bound to be distraught waiting on us."

On her way back to the door, Rosemary attempted to hide her shaking hands, thrusting them into the pockets of her cardigan. She was surprised to discover one side wasn't empty; it contained several smooth, round objects.

Rosemary couldn't fathom how her pocket had come to be filled with a handful of marbles, but then she remembered Lionel's pawing and realized he must have deposited them there during his butterscotch search.

She stopped short as she rounded the corner, and there peeking out from the coat cupboard was a familiar-looking piece of fabric. A hideous shade of pea green, rubberized to keep its wearer dry, it was the same color as the raincoat that had served as the last piece of evidence against Lottie Lewis.

What had been only a suspicion turned Rosemary's stomach to acid. She took a deep breath while her eyes went saucer-wide, and she realized she'd not been so far out of Father Dawson's murder investigation as she'd thought. Here she was again, solving the case, even though she'd tried her best to avoid becoming involved.

Keep your head, Rosemary said to herself, but a strange sensation traveled the length of her spine and caused her to glance furtively around. It was then she saw Cleo, in the mirror over the fireplace, watching her with hawk-like eyes.

She wasn't sure when she'd been made, but in Cleo's hands was a knife, the edge gleaming in the light shining through the sitting room window. "Not so fast," she said, deadpan.

Rosemary glanced at the door, wondering if she could outrun the old woman, but realized with a sinking feeling there wouldn't be time.

Cleo let out an evil-sounding laugh that gripped Rosemary's heart like an icy fist. Whatever was she going to do now?

Chapter Nineteen

Rosemary put her hands in the air and turned slowly around. "Mrs. Holmes, what—what are you doing?" she stuttered, realizing a second too late how cliche the question sounded.

"Are you daft? I'm protecting myself, of course. Can't have you running off to that inspector, telling him everything you saw. I knew you were trouble from the first time I laid eyes on you."

Dash watched the exchange from his perch on the settee. Rosemary thought it seemed as though he understood the conversation between her and Cleo. It only took a moment for her to realize she must be in some kind of a shock to have had such a foolish idea.

"I don't know what you're talking about," she said meekly, trying again to backtrack.

Cleo wasn't buying it, but stalling allowed precious seconds for Rosemary to formulate a plan.

"Why did you do it?" She asked, changing tack. "By all

counts, you cared for Father Dawson a great deal. What could he possibly have done to make you turn against him?"

The knife wavered slightly, but then Cleo's face settled into stone. "You must think *I'm* entirely daft," she spat, flicking a glance towards the mantle and the vicar's portrait.

"Ah," Rosemary said knowingly as she made a split-second decision to play out her hunch. "You loved him, didn't you? Desperately, by the looks of it. And he didn't love you. I'm sorry. It's difficult to be overlooked. Especially when the object of one's affection chooses an unworthy mate. Lottie Lewis didn't deserve Father Dawson's favor, did she?"

It was a desperate attempt to get Cleo talking and buy herself some time, and Rosemary breathed an internal sigh of relief when it seemed her ploy was working.

Cleo kept the knife raised and steady, but she faltered, and Rosemary knew she'd found her in. Belle Dawson had posed the question: what girl wants to be thrown over? Now, Cleo Holmes was proving the answer was none. Not even a girl of fifty-plus years.

"Tell me," Rosemary cajoled. "You can either kill me, or we can both walk away from this. If you kill me, at least I can die knowing why. If not, then you should convince me why I shouldn't go to the police. Why Lottie

Lewis should take the blame. Either way, confession soothes the weary soul, does it not?"

If there was one thing Rosemary knew, it was that murderers always wanted their cunning to be known, at least by someone. Cleo seemed to want to fight that urge, so onward, Rosemary pressed.

"Let me see if I've got it right," she said thoughtfully, her eyes flicking to the collection of oil paintings she'd admired earlier. "You like it here, in your little house so close to the vicarage and the object of your affection. Watching what's going on over there is like your own personal stage production. Lottie *was* there. You weren't lying about that. Belle can corroborate."

Rosemary tried to think two steps ahead, sort out all the pieces of the puzzle correctly. "It stands to reason the argument was truth as well. Fergus wasn't lying, either. The dog he heard was, of course, Dash. You crept over to the vicarage to eavesdrop, didn't you?"

"I went over there to make sure Father Dawson was all right!" Cleo finally snapped and corrected Rosemary's assumption. She'd struck a nerve, and now that she had, she wasn't sure her plan had been the best laid.

"Dash was all up in a tizzy. He could hear Lottie screeching all the way from here. So, I grabbed my umbrella and took the path towards the vicarage. I'd only gotten halfway there when I heard Lottie telling Father

Dawson he'd given his girl too much leeway. She said Belle was spoiled and treated everyone, including him, with disrespect. He simply replied that Belle deserved understanding. She'd had a hard life, he tried to explain, but Lottie would have none of it!"

None of this came as a shock to Rosemary. Father Dawson, as she'd proclaimed to Vera, doted on his daughter. It must have been quite frustrating for Lottie, and her having finally snapped wasn't such an outrageous scenario.

"Then she left, didn't she?" Rosemary pressed.

"She did! She told him she knew he would always choose Belle over her, said it was over between them, and she left." The memory seemed to please Cleo, but her wicked smile quickly turned sour.

"After her car rumbled down the drive, that stupid dog," Cleo glared at Dash, "got loose and ran straight through the vicarage garden and into the graveyard. I had no choice but to follow and try to catch the little beast."

"And that's when you lost the umbrella," Rosemary finished. She sensed they were coming to the climax of the story, which meant she didn't have much time to spare. A quick glance around the sitting room told her that the fireplace poker was her best chance of weapon, except that it was too close to Cleo to be considered a viable option.

"I didn't lose it," Cleo snapped. "I simply set it down. At that point, there had been a lull in the storm. I didn't need the umbrella anymore, so I rested it carefully against the gate. Do you know how much that thing cost me? What I so loved about it turned out to be a curse in disguise. Had I chosen a basic black style, nobody would have ever been the wiser. But plum? I don't know what I was thinking."

Having followed her thoughts down the path of a tangent, Cleo waved the knife around as she talked. Rosemary felt a flare of hope well in her chest. Cleo's attention had been split. *If only*, Rosemary thought and pressed on.

"Is that when you summoned Father Dawson?" she prodded, inching closer to the door. "Or did he hear Dash's bark and venture out into the night?" She didn't know how much longer she might have before Vera sent a search party, and the last thing she wanted was anyone else put in harm's way.

"Yes, yes, that was it," Cleo answered, her eyes turning somewhat misty even as her hand tightened around the hilt of the knife. "Dash raced over to the vicar and danced around his feet. He never comes when I call. Quite often, he runs the other way, but all Horatio had to do was whistle. That's when—that's when"—

Rosemary merely nodded now. Cleo needed no further

prompting, so caught up she was in her reverie.

"I thanked him and said, 'Dash simply adores you,' to which he replied, 'And I, him. I adore all of God's creatures.' I couldn't keep the rest from tumbling out. I asked Father Dawson if he could ever love me. My heart had belonged to him for so long—long before Lottie Lewis decided to swoop in and claim him for her own!"

It wasn't an appropriate thought or a particularly helpful one, but Rosemary had to stifle a nervous giggle from rising in her throat at the prospect of an aging vicar such as Father Dawson having possessed the gravitas to affect so many of his female parishioners so profoundly.

She sobered quickly when that train of thought led to the realization that it was precisely Father Dawson's gravitas that had gotten him murdered, the fingers of her right hand closed around the contents of her cardigan pocket.

Rosemary didn't need to hear Cleo's next comment to know she'd been rebuffed. Having met the vicar, she guessed he'd let the woman down as gently as he could but unfortunately for him, it hadn't changed his fate.

"I don't know what came over me," Cleo lamented now. "Rage roared in my heart. I hadn't felt that much pain since my Barty passed away. I don't remember exactly what happened then, but the next thing I knew, Father Dawson wasn't breathing. I pulled the raincoat sash from around his neck and tried to revive him. It wasn't until I realized it was too late that I noticed Dash was gone—and so was the sash. None of this would have happened if it weren't for that bloody dog!"

Cleo lunged now, and several things happened at once.

First, Rosemary pulled her hand out of her pocket and flung a handful of marbles as hard as she could. They pelted her attacker's head and face before showering to the floor in a clatter, causing Cleo to scream and drop the knife.

Second—and this one came as a shock to Rosemary as well as Cleo—the front door burst open to reveal the last person anyone would have ever expected to come to her rescue: Fergus Poole.

"You killed Father Dawson!" he screamed at Cleo, kicking the knife away and pinning her to the ground, "and my statement helped you get away with it!"

"Fergus," Rosemary cried, "don't do anything rash! She's not worth it."

He scowled at Rosemary and growled, "I'm not going to stoop to her level. I want to hear her admit it!"

"And you shall, dear boy, but you must keep your wits," Rosemary advised, calmer than she ought to have been. Perhaps being faced, regularly, with deranged murderers had numbed her somewhat to the excitement.

Fergus took a deep breath and looked to Rosemary with

wide eyes as though the reality of the situation had just occurred to him. Before he could begin to panic, she turned and made one last jab at Cleo.

"You probably thought luck had shined on you when both Belle and Fergus came forward and told the police what they knew about Lottie," she prodded. "But Lottie wasn't lying, was she? She did come back later that night. Otherwise, she wouldn't have heard Hyacinth and Alistair Cox in the graveyard. That was a problem, but Alistair's outstanding warrants kept him from offering a statement, and the girl he was with certainly wouldn't offer herself up as a suspect."

When Dash yipped once, and instead of choosing his master, came to sit at Rosemary's feet, another piece of the puzzle fell into place.

"You've been trying to catch Dash all week, not because you wanted your little Dashy-do back, but because you hoped he'd lead you back to the murder weapon," she said.

With Fergus seated firmly on her back, Cleo's voice sounded a bit breathless. "Fool dog. He gets hold of something and won't stop playing with it until he's ready. I chased him all over town."

While Cleo spilled more of the details, Rosemary opened the coat cupboard and felt around for another one with a belt. It was only fitting, she thought, for Cleo to be trussed up good and proper with something very like the thing she'd used to kill a good man.

"Fergus, if you wouldn't mind taking charge of Mrs. Homes, I have a wedding to attend, and I believe a certain inspector will be quite pleased to hear your version of what happened here today. I'll send him directly the moment I see him."

"I'd be right honored to tell him." None too gently, Fergus took the second belt Rosemary had found and bound Cleo's feet as well.

As Rosemary made to leave, Dash pranced around her feet, circling and leaping, his bright eyes a mute plea. Not entirely mute, as he yipped several times. She leaned down, petted his domed head, and asked Fergus one more favor. When she returned to the Blackburn house, the dog would be there waiting for her.

Rosemary smoothed her hair as she walked quickly back to the church. Frederick poked his head out of the double doors and shot her a scathing look.

"We were just about to send a search party," he exclaimed irritably. "Where have you been?"

Leave it to Frederick to admonish her when she'd just spent the last half hour fighting for her life. Not to mention, his search party would have arrived mere moments too late. Her brother's timing never had been

214

ideal.

"Mother reports that Vera found…whatever it was she was looking for shortly after you left," he continued, waving her inside.

"One second," Rosemary said as she caught sight of Inspector Trousseau seated near the very rear of the bride's side of the nave.

She crept along until she was directly behind him and then surreptitiously tapped him on the shoulder. When he turned, surprised, she leaned in and whispered, "Cleo Holmes murdered Father Dawson. She's just confessed. Fergus Poole has her trussed up in her sitting room. This *lady detective* thinks it would be prudent of you to arrest her—and let Lottie Lewis walk free."

Before he could reply, she sauntered off, a satisfied smile spreading across her face. *That would teach him*, she thought smugly.

Chapter Twenty

When Vera stepped into view, a collective sigh rippled across the church. She paused for a moment, her smile as radiant as the sun, her arm gently resting on that of Cecil Woolridge.

At some point during the week, Evelyn and Vera had put their heads together and decided Rosemary's father should be the one to walk the bride down the aisle. Vera had, Evelyn pointed out, spent enough time with the family to be considered an honorary member even before she and Frederick made the union legal.

For his part, Cecil played the proud papa times two with great dignity, whispering something to her as he handed Vera off to his son, that even to Rosemary, she never would repeat.

In a pool of afternoon light, which Vera would later begrudgingly admit, had shined in through the stained-glass windows with a soft glow that only served to enhance the beaded detail of her dress, Frederick took her to be his wife. If the bride's voice hesitated slightly at the vow to obey her husband, it was only to be expected from those who knew her well.

Rosemary never asked, nor did she want to know, by what method Kit managed to overcome his fear of speaking in front of strangers, but she sincerely hoped it hadn't included the imagining of anyone naked.

When he asked Vera if she would "take this man to be your lawfully wedded husband?" Rosemary thought her heart might burst with happiness. The pure joy on Frederick's face when she replied with a resounding, "I do," let loose the waterworks.

It wasn't only Rosemary; she doubted there was a dry eye in the house—except for maybe Simon's. Supposedly, according to Frederick, he'd sworn off women entirely after his adventure at the pub.

Later, during the reception, Kit approached Vera and Rosemary, who stood watching Frederick dance with his mother while his father squired Lorraine around the floor.

"I wanted to thank you," Kit said, clasping Vera's hand tightly, "for your encouragement, however unorthodox it may have been. I faced my fear of the stage, and it was quite freeing. My path, now, is clear," he explained, his glance traveling momentarily across the room to rest on

Belle Dawson. "I almost ended up married to a woman I would not have chosen for myself."

"What will happen to Belle now?" Vera prodded.

"Mrs. Melville offered to take her in, but Belle refused. I believe Mrs. Woolridge has offered her a position in her husband's offices, so she will be moving to London."

"Come again?" This was news that shocked Rosemary into speaking.

"Belle has been handling all of the vicar's correspondence for some time now. She writes with a clear hand and has a knack for organizing church documents that should stand her in good stead for secretarial work."

"It seems my mother has been quite busy arranging people's lives all week."

"Or she's forcing Cecil to pay penance for letting things go at the house," Vera offered just before being called away at the behest of another group of well-wishers.

"And what will you do now?" Left standing, Rosemary asked Kit. "Will you take over for Father Dawson officially?"

"I shall attempt to fill his shoes," he answered, his attention focused on someone or something just past Rosemary's left ear. She turned her head to see what it might be and found herself looking at Delilah. The girl cleaned up nicely, Rosemary thought. Kit, it seemed, thought so as well. "If you'll excuse me, there's someone I must speak with."

Curious, Rosemary watched Delilah's face go from sullen to mildly surprised to that indefinable look a woman gets when she realizes the man of her dreams is interested in her.

"I give it three months," said a voice near Rosemary's ear. She turned to see Hyacinth standing there.

"Delilah may not have the most sparkling personality, but surely Kit has more fortitude than that."

"No, I mean until they're married. You know I shall tease her without mercy." Hyacinth began to repeat Delilah's speech on how she planned never to wed but stopped when a hand landed on her shoulder.

"Excuse me, Miss Hyacinth, but would you honor me with a dance?" Fergus blushed and swallowed hard, but he managed the invitation despite his nerves.

"I…" Hyacinth stammered, "Yes, I suppose I would." She went off, leaving Rosemary to look for Max. Scanning the crowd, she found him across the way in earnest conversation with her father.

"It will be your turn again next," Lorraine sounded ever-so-slightly sloshed as she slung an arm around Rosemary, drew her in for a sideways hug. "He's a good man." Being observant when it came to men, she'd noticed the direction of Rosemary's gaze.

"Sooner, rather than later, I hope." Rosemary's mother had taken her place on Rosemary's other side. "I would very much like to dandle another grandchild on my knee."

Arguing with two mothers at a wedding wasn't a good use of anyone's time, so Rosemary merely said, "I'll take that under advisement. Now, I think I shall go rescue Max from father."

As the car carrying Frederick and Vera pulled out of sight, Rosemary let out a tired sigh and sagged against Max's side. "That's done," she said. "It was a lovely wedding, but I'm glad it's over."

"I could sleep for a week," Max certainly gave the appearance of a man who had not rested well for quite some time. "And, if you don't mind me saying, I've had enough of Pardington to last me for a while."

Whatever had gone on at Woolridge House while the women were away? On second thought, Rosemary decided she'd rather not know.

"What would you say," Max continued as he swung her into a loose embrace, "to the idea of driving back to London tonight?"

Gazing into his eyes, she smiled and said, "Yes, Max. I would like very much to spend a night in my own bed. There's only one thing I feel I must share. I have a new man in my life, and I only hope he will not turn out to hog the blankets."

"Who? What?" Max gave her shoulders the merest shake. "I don't understand. I thought we were, I mean to say—." Shock and dismay turned his features to a mask of disbelief.

"Shh, it's not what you think, darling, but it is time you met Dash."

-The End-

Don't miss the next book in the Mrs. Lillywhite Investigates series: *A Twisted Case of Murder*

28828823R00132